LIE TO ME

LIE TO ME

A Novel

DAVID SMALL

Tosca Books

Some of the material in this book originally appeared in a different form in ALONE, published in 1991 by W. W. Norton. It has been rewritten and repurposed thematically for the present book.

Lyrics from "Don Gato," Copyright 1964, 1971, 1988 by Silver Burdett & Ginn. All rights reserved. Used with permission.

Special thanks to Bryson Design and Studio 530.

Other books by David Small

Almost Famous
The River in Winter
Alone
More of Everything: A Love Story

To Jemry and Dennison

With Thanks to Frankie, Deborah, and Neil

And in Loving Memory of
Elisabeth and Robert Russell

I

CHAPTER | ONE

I met Linda Gagliano in the fall of 1977 when we were both students at Parkman College, a small liberal arts school located in the little artsy town of Columbus, Pennsylvania. If I had stayed to talk to Professor Robinson a few minutes longer that morning, I might never have met her and my life would have been entirely different. It's also possible that a few people I've known would still be alive today. But on that long ago October day, when I unwittingly glanced over my shoulder at the dark haired pretty girl bouncing down the steps of the college library as I was going up, I had no premonition what I was letting myself in for, no idea that a glimpse in the wrong direction could end so disastrously.

She was so attractive and lively that my eyes automatically followed her to see where all that energy was taking her. To the backseat window of a black limousine parked at the curb, as it turned out--a long dark sinister-looking machine, malevolently idling there, that somehow I hadn't noticed. She was wearing a red sweater, a white Alpaca scarf trailing down her back, a tight black and white dogtooth print skirt which cupped her backside nicely, and she was clutching her hands together and jumping excitedly up and down in front of the black glass window as it slowly slid down, releasing an unwinding serpent of blue cigar smoke. A gnarled hand the color of walnut passed her a thick manila envelope. Squealing with delight, she stuck her head through the smoke and kissed the apparition inside, barely escaping being guillotined before the window slid shut and the car started for the gates. She was still jumping up and down with excitement, only now she was waving the thick envelope at the back of the retreating car.

I heard her trill, "Bye! Thanks, Daddy!"

Only after the car slipped through the college gates and disappeared into the real world did she turn and see me standing there, staring at her with my mouth open.

"Hey! Flycatcher!"

I looked around to make sure she meant me.

"You wanna catch a cup of coffee?"

I had never seen anybody get what I assumed was a thick package of money (rightly, as it turned out) through a lowered car window. I wanted to know more about this lucky girl. I trailed after her to the student union. She could have put a ring in my nose and led me there by a chain, I was that beguiled by this darkly pretty fine-boned girl. Over our coffee, she told me she was from Long Island. When I looked blank—there were a lot of long islands in the world, and I was trying to remember the name of the one where Circe changed men into pigs—she said, "Long Island, baby. New York? Where some of the best looking women on the planet live?"

"I'm beginning to realize that."

She grinned and asked my name. When I told her it was Earl, she played it for a laugh out of the side of her mouth like Joan Rivers cracking wise.

"Maybe there's a silver lining here, Earl. What's your middle name?"

"Ray. Earl Ray Bogwell, Jr. My dad goes by Ray. So naturally--"

"What! Are you from West Virginia? I'm getting mixed up with some kind of hucklebuck here!"

Although she was trying for funny, I should have realized right then that she knew how to punch where it hurt. I hated my name. It was a knot in the middle of my personality that I would spend years trying to untangle. As soon as I figured out my true identity, I planned on changing it to something more suitable. (I thought

"Steve" would be nice.) But despite the little twinge of pain that she'd induced with her smart-ass remarks about my name, I was dazzled. I liked her sassiness, the comic way she'd dabbed a little saltiness in my wounds. After about twenty minutes she said, "Hey, I gotta go."

"How about insulting me some more on Friday night?"

"Insulting you some more?"

"I'd like to take you to that pizza joint on Vine and buy you a slice and a Coke."

"How cute. Like a date?"

"Right. Like a date."

"You sure about this?"

"What? Sure I'm sure."

"I mean, I can insult you without going on a date with you."

"I know, but let's make it official, like a date, okay?"

"Okay, Billy Bob! You're on!"

On Friday night at six, I found her waiting for me on the steps outside her apartment building. She had the collar of her pea jacket turned up and a matching woolen watch cap crushed down on her curls--curls black and shiny as crow's feathers, her fists doubled in her pockets. She presented a lovely silhouette against the darkening sky. In that moment she could have passed as a model for a fashion house that used glammed up street urchins on its runways.

When I walked up, she tossed me her car keys.

"You drive."

"The pizza place is around the corner. Why don't we walk?"

"We're not going there, dummy. I got something better in mind for you."

Her car was parked behind the building. It turned out to be a 1959 Karmann Ghia, in the beautiful color the Volkswagen people call "Pacific Blue"; it was the coupe with the low taillights the way Luigi Segre had intended. It was an absolute masterpiece of design that belonged in MOMA, not in the hands of a college kid. I couldn't believe I knew someone who actually owned one.

"Wow. It's beautifully restored."

"Not restored. It's out of the box original. Daddy bought it for me the year I was born. It's been up on blocks in the garage at home. Daddy's Cousin Vito kept it polished and nice for me. Daddy decided I was old enough to drive it this semester. It's only got four thousand miles on it."

I couldn't believe my luck. Here I was, driving the car of my adolescent fantasies with a beautiful girl leaning into me with her arm on my leg, smiling at me as I did my best to look like an expert driver behind the two spoke steering wheel, trying not to grind the four speed manual gear box into metal filings.

"You like this car?"

"I certainly do."

She leaned back in her seat, satisfied with my answer, having apparently decided that despite my ridiculous name I wasn't a complete doofus. She directed me to the most expensive restaurant in town. I sat in excruciating torment all through dinner, wondering how in God's name I was going to break it to her that I only had twenty dollars in my wallet. I broke out in a sweat when she ordered filet mignon for both of us, shrimp cocktail to start, crème brulée for dessert. The dinner was fantastic, we were getting along fine, and apart from feeling damned to spending the rest of my life busing tables and washing dishes to pay the tab for this meal, I had another worry, a ripple of uneasiness, when I noticed two men at a nearby table watching us while they pretended not to. One of them had a huge forehead and the sad face of a donkey; the other had a shaved head that looked hard as a bullet. Why the interest in us? I did my best to ignore them. It was unsettling and ruined my attempt to impress her by explaining how much I knew about *Paradise Lost*, which I hadn't actually read. I don't know why she didn't stand up and yell, "Time's up!" and turn the evening into a speed date, but she continued to sit there and look at me like I had two heads.

"Gee, you must be smart."

The sarcasm in that remark eluded me. When the bill came, to my shamefaced relief, she swooped on it like a bird of prey. She extracted two one hundred dollar bills from that thick envelope she was still carrying in her purse. I had never seen a hundred dollar bill before. It looked fake, too crisp and bright green to be real. I was astonished when the waiter accepted them without hesitation and brought her a pile of normal-looking change on a pewter salver. When she dropped a fifty on the plate for the waiter's tip, she said, with feigned innocence, "You think that's enough?"

Over her shoulder, I watched the man with the shaved head intercept the waiter and take the fifty off the plate and replace it with a bill out of his pocket and jerk his head to one side as if telling the waiter to scram. The waiter, looking scared, did as he was told. The man shoved the fifty in his pocket and gave me a hard steely look as if to say, *You want to make something of it?* Then after having pinned me to my seat with a look I'll never forget, he turned away from me with an air of contempt and he and Donkey Man walked unhurriedly out of the restaurant. From the looks of their table, they'd only ordered a pitcher of water. They had sat there playing with their napkins, drinking water, and feigning indifference while keeping us under surveillance. Linda saw the look on my face and asked me what was wrong. I told her nothing was wrong, everything was fine. She studied me for a beat under her dark eyebrows.

"You should learn to relax."

"I'm relaxed," I lied. "I'm always relaxed."

I expected to get rolled in the parking lot. They'd seen the thick envelope of money she had waved around when the bill came, but there was no sign of them outside. I kept my eye on the rear view mirror as I drove her back to her apartment but, so far as I could tell, nobody followed us.

To say that I was impressed with everything that happened that night (even the shake down of the waiter and the high anxiety of possibly getting sapped in the parking lot) would be an understatement. That included the punch on the nose Linda gave me when I tried to French kiss her as we said goodnight.

"Not so fast, buster!"

She gave me a hell of a shot; then wiped away the hurt expression on my face with a kiss on my cheek.

"Let your imagination work on that."

Then added, "You know, this is the first date I've been on in about a year at this crummy college? You seem like a nice guy. Maybe we'll do it again."

I didn't tell her we had that in common. Pretty and vivacious with curves in all the right places, this girl should have had no problem getting a date. It made no sense to me. Without another word, she disappeared into her apartment house. Having no other option (getting laid was out) I turned up the collar of my jacket and walked back through the dark star-lit night and an increasingly sharp wind to the rooms that I shared with Arthur Frankenwood, the Belle of the Ball. I don't mean to say that Arthur was gay, just that he was extremely popular and I was not. Since I'd never been on a date in the five semesters we'd roomed together, the minute I came in the door he wanted to hear all about it. After all, it was an astonishing development, comparable in his mind to the discovery of another planet circling the sun. Arthur knew everyone on campus and could tell you what business their fathers were in and how much money they had, down to the last zero. He dated some of the most attractive women on campus, always off with them to rock concerts and the theater in New York. His father had money; mine did not. I led the impoverished social life of a Cistercian monk, barely opening my mouth from one day to the next. I knew few people outside of the English Department. My idea of a night out was a beer and an anchovy salad at a bar in town called the Rose Bowl with a paperback of Browning's "The Ring and the Book" for company. Why Arthur had picked me for a roommate in our freshman year was one of life's little mysteries. Somehow we'd become good friends, finding strength, if not amusement, in our mutual incompatibility. Also I think he enjoyed pitying me. He had my future down as one of teaching library science at a second-rate university. Clearly an ambitious young man, he had nothing to fear from me. That night, we opened a couple of beers and sat down to talk. I told him I thought I had met the girl of my dreams--or my nightmares, I wasn't sure which.

"Who is this enthralling creature?"

When I told him, he actually turned white.

"You poor sap! Nobody goes *near* that girl. Her father's a mobster."

"Don't hand me that baloney. I'm not buying."

"No baloney. In crime circles he's known as 'Phil the Barber.'"

"Phil the Barber! What a crock!"

He told me two stories intended to raise the hair on my neck. The first involved a salesman who didn't understand that Linda's family held the wholesale concession for selling supplies to barbershops and salons throughout the Tri-State Area. When this poor deluded soul persisted in trying to persuade shops to buy his stuff, he had ended up in the trunk of his car at Jamaica Raceway with a bullet in the back of his head and a bottle of hair tonic shoved up his ass.

"You made that up, Arthur."

"You think so? Ask Linda."

The other story involved a boy named Jeremy Bigelow whom Linda had dated in her freshman year. They'd had a fight one night and when she slapped him, Jeremy made the mistake of slapping her back. Six weeks later, he was "mugged" by a couple of men in suits who seemed less interested in his watch and his wallet than beating the crap out of him. When one of them noticed he was wearing a Timex, and looked in his wallet and saw he only had twenty-three dollars, they laughed as though it was a big joke and gave him a few extra kicks in the ribs. They took his watch and wallet anyway. The "loot" if you want to call it that, including the bills, was later recovered in a nearby creek. Jeremy ended in the hospital with a broken jaw, several missing teeth, smashed ribs, a punctured lung, and a fractured leg. He never returned to campus. His parents came down to school and packed up his room with the hurried furtiveness of thieves in the night. The minute he could manage crutches, Jeremy fled the hospital, never to be seen near the college (or Linda) again.

"Come on, Arthur. This is total bullshit."

"Right. Remember how you laughed it off when the old man's goons wrap you in cement and drop you in the East River."

We laughed like a couple of hyenas, neither of us believing what he was saying. It was only later that I remembered what Linda said when I asked her out: *You sure about this?* After my talk with Arthur, it sounded a lot more ominous. When I think of the dizzying twists and turns that followed that evening, ending dressed in a suit of cement was only one possibility. Frankly, I am amazed that I am here telling you this story; amazed that I am still able to walk (no baseball bat to the kneecaps); talk (no pliers, followed by a boning knife to the tongue); and see out of both eyes (no eyeball flipped out with a pocketknife). I don't mean to alarm you. These are horribly violent images, I know; but in some dark corners of the human psyche, they pass for the language of love.

CHAPTER | TWO

Linda wanted me to go home with her over the Thanksgiving break and meet her family and I was all for it. I had no desire to go home and see my parents, Ray and Nola, where holidays were either a drag, or a trial, depending on how crazy they were acting, but my brother Richie was coming home for a short visit and I badly wanted to see him. He hadn't graced us with his presence since he flunked out of the football program at Eastern Missouri three years ago. I say he flunked out of the football program because that's what he was there for, not the academics. He'd been redshirted and told he was too small to play quarterback because he couldn't see over his linemen. After a year and a half of humiliation and what he considered unfair treatment he'd quit. Since then, he'd gotten his pilot's license and was flying air freight for a small airline out of Tampa Bay, Florida.

Richie was everything I wasn't. Voted the most popular boy in his class, one of the leading high school quarterbacks in Pennsylvania, all state in baseball, and second team in basketball, despite being 5' 9." He was handsome and charismatic, and all the girls loved him. I wanted to know how he felt about being a normal human instead of a super athlete. I thought I might be gaining on him now that I had a girlfriend with what I considered was a glamorous background. I loved him, but I badly wanted to beat him at something. I had always been the back up kid, the bench warmer brother, in our family. Ray and Nola had taken pride in Richie's athletic accomplishments; it was something that made sense, something tangible and real. They had thick scrapbooks filled with his heroics to prove it. During his high school years, the house was always lively with his teammates, big good looking humble boys and their pretty girlfriends. There were parties and music in the house after games. It was an exciting time. Now that his star had darkened, so had their lives. I offered them little by way of consolation, a few poems published in the college's literary annual. Hardly the stuff to set them cheering.

The big thing was to see him and afterwards get out of there as quickly as possible. Linda and I worked it out that her father would send Cousin Vito down to school with the car and drive her back to the Island, and I would follow the day after Thanksgiving in her Karmann Ghia. She had mentioned Cousin Vito several times, but when he got out of the limo at precisely the appointed time of ten-thirty the Tuesday morning before Thanksgiving, he didn't look anything like I'd pictured. He was tall and skinny, with a thin covering of black threads stitched into his skull, and looked like a cadaverous version of Boris Karloff. He was dressed in black-even his shirt and tie were black. I would learn he always dressed in black, always ready for a funeral, should one pop up, his pants held up by white suspenders. When he came around the car and saw me standing there holding Linda's suitcase, he whipped off his sunglasses and put his hand inside his jacket, with a sour look of surprise on his face like an old man mistaking indigestion for a heart attack.

"Wha', who's dis?"

"It's okay," Linda put a hand on his arm as he stared at me like a hawk eyeing a rabbit. "This is Earl, my boyfriend."

He flashed his yellow fangs at me in a sort of Bela Lugosi smile. I can't help using monsters to describe this man. Although he turned out to be a sweetheart, you could see from the shadows behind his ravaged eyes and the cruel lines around his mouth that he must have been a different, possibly dangerous, person as a young man.

"Oh, yeah. I heard about you. Get in. Mr. Gagliano wants to see you."

He clutched my arm and started moving me toward the car.

"No, no, Cousin Vito. He's not coming with us. He's driving my car to the Island after he has Thanksgiving with his family. Remember?"

"Sure, I remember now. Lemme take that," and ripped the suitcase out of my hand. Linda gave me a peck on the cheek and got in the car and they were off, Linda waving frantically out the back window at me like she'd just been kidnapped.

I went home feeling both bereft and relieved, experiencing the same fugue of ambiguity that I'd had about her ever since my talk with Arthur. I thought I loved her, but I was a little scared of her, too.

When I pulled into the driveway of our split-level brick ranch house with the gold-colored metal shingles that some huckster had talked Ray into, there was Richie by the back door with our fat old collie dogs waiting for me, a grin on his face as wide as a football field. We greeted each other with the usual horseplay: punches to the gut, cuffing each other around the head and shoulders. My head was still ringing and my eyes blind with tears both from the pounding he'd given me and the sheer emotion at seeing him again, when he asked me where I got the car. I told him it belonged to my girl.

"You have a girl? The little scholar has a girl? Can you beat that?" and clapped me on the back so hard if I'd had false teeth like Ray they would have flown out of my mouth and knocked out one of the dogs. I told him I was only sticking around for Thanksgiving. The day after, I was driving to Long Island to meet my girl's family.

"Wow. Sounds serious. I don't blame you for getting out of here. I've been here a day, and it's already too long. I only stuck around to see you. Me, I'm leaving on Friday too. Ma's made a big scene about it, but I'm outta here."

"How are they?"

"Buggy as ever."

We went in the house. Nola was at the kitchen table in her pajamas and robe, looking wounded, and suffered me to give her a kiss on the cheek.

"Hi, Ma."

"Well, isn't this nice. Both my boys taking a few minutes out of their busy lives to spend with their mother."

Ray stood up and shook my hand. He was flushed and smelled of booze.

"Now that the gang's all here, let's have a drink."

He'd made baked beans and a cabbage salad for dinner, and we had a relatively peaceful time of it that evening. Ray was pleasantly drunk and well behaved in honor of our homecoming. Nola took a few verbal jabs at her thankless children and stayed awake long enough to play a couple of hands of Crazy Eights with us before she retired to her alternate universe. At the end of the evening Ray opened the refrigerator to show me the twenty-pound turkey he'd bought at the farmers' market.

"We'll plan on dinner at noon. I'll pop it in the oven at seven. That'll be plenty of time. I'll set my alarm for six-thirty. Let's have a nightcap and call it a day."

We were all drunk. Richie and I didn't want a drink but we didn't want to upset him by refusing, so we had another drink and staggered off to our respective rooms, trailed by the dogs. I woke up around eleven the next morning with a terrific headache. The house was filled with the cottony silence of a funeral parlor. I went into Richie's room but the corpse was missing. I could see him out the window down by the horse barn. He was leaning on the white board fence, brooding over the horses he had let out into the pasture. I went upstairs and found Ray sitting at the kitchen table in front of some of his favorite formaldehyde.

"We'll be having dinner a little later than I planned," he said. "I forgot to get up. I'll call Richie in and we'll get your mother out of her pod and have a little breakfast. Sound good?"

He went out on the deck and called Richie into the house, and while Richie and I went into Nola's bedroom and raised her from the dead, Ray mixed himself another drink, his third or fourth of the day. We sat her down in a bleary-eyed stupor on the old brown velour couch in the living room. She was dressed in a pair of ancient silk pajamas that Ray's mother had given him one Christmas eons ago, the navy blue ones with the red piping raveling out in places; and over the top of these she'd pulled on his threadbare old yellowy-white terry cloth bathrobe with the cigarette burns all over it. She hadn't combed her hair. She sat there, her feet tucked under her, looking fat and slack in Ray's old bedclothes. Ray put some croissants in the microwave, set up some TV trays, made Nola an Old Fashioned, and served us what passed for breakfast at Chez Bogwell. I turned on the oven and stuck the bird in so at least we had that going. Nola was so numbed over with sleeping pills and tranquilizers she could hardly hold her head up.

"Where you going, Ma? Back to Coo-Coo Cloudland?"

Her nebulous blue eyes fluttered open again. She smiled at Richie, her adorable, her beautiful first-born boy, who had once driven Apollo's horses to heaven's zenith and might do it again someday if the gods were kind, and now he was home from the clouds, still marked for greatness by Zeus's invisible eagle on his shoulder, his hair tied back with golden grasshoppers, signs that only Nola could see. She fumbled around with her glass until she found the top of the end table.

"Land sakes, I can't seem to keep my eyes open today."

"Come on, Ma. I'll get you a cup of coffee. You can take a nap later."

Ray made the mistake of putting in his two cents.

"Give it a try, Nole. Hell, the boys are home and it's Thanksgiving."

"I know what day it is, thank you."

This remark used up the last of her strength. Her eyelids fluttered a few more times; her head rolled back and then forward; and slowly she subsided to the cushions. We watched this performance with the attention of experts. In two minutes, she was out cold. When she started to snore, we moved to the kitchen. We sat at the kitchen table drinking beer, and kidded Ray about how he couldn't say, "Electricity."

"You always say 'electwisity' instead of "electricity."

"I do not."

"Yes, you do, Dad. You talk like Elmer Fudd. 'Where did that pesky wabbit go?'"

"'Dwat that wabbit.'"

We rocked from side to side, like Ray Charles at the keyboard, and laughed until the tears ran down our faces. Ray sat there smiling thinly as if to say: Wait until it's my turn.

"What say we play a little golf? I want to show you this thing. I'll bring it up from downstairs. Wait 'til you see this."

He went downstairs to the game room and brought up a box and his bag of clubs. We went in the living room. Nola was flat on her back, her eyes fluttering, her mouth open in the shape of the universal mantra, apparently communing with the spirit world. Ray ignored her and unpacked his putting green. We moved some furniture out of the way and he rolled out the green.

"What do you think, boys?"

It was impressive. It was a lovely mossy color, six feet by ten, three cups on the far edges and a hole in the center. It was configured to have some natural breaks so you could truly work on your putting and chip shots. For a while everything went well. Richie was regularly making his shots and Ray was regularly missing his. Ray finished Nola's Old Fashioned, then started drinking his bourbon straight. Richie and I stuck with beer, because it looked like it was going to be a long night. Around five o'clock, I went in the kitchen to peel some potatoes and chop some carrots and discovered Ray had turned off the oven.

"We're going out to dinner," he said. "No point hanging around here."

"We can't leave Ma."

"Yes, we can. She won't even know we're gone."

As if the emphasize the point, he got out one of his woods, teed the ball on his putting mat and hit it as hard as he could. The ball knocked a chunk out of the lamp on the end table above Nola's head and ricocheted off the far wall. He teed up again and this time put a crack in the picture window at the end of the room.

He turned around and smiled at us.

"See?"

We did see. She hadn't flinched or moved an inch.

We drove down the hill into town to Clyde Monroe's restaurant at seventy miles an hour in Ray's El Dorado. It was like going down a chute on a toboggan. Richie was rolling around in the back, cackling like a fool.

At the restaurant, Ray ordered us a big spread and then excused himself. We watched him weave across the floor, lightly touching the tables and shoulders of other diners, attracting their somber stares, as he unsteadily made his way to the swinging doors at the back of the room.

"What's he up to?"

"Only God knows. Even He isn't sure."

Eventually Clyde came out of the kitchen and solved the mystery, or at least part of it. He told us that Ray had suddenly remembered an urgent appointment and had gone out the back door.

We looked out the window. The El Dorado was gone.

"Meal's all paid for, boys. Enjoy. I'll give you a lift home afterwards."

"You still have all your waitresses, Clyde?"

"He wasn't after waitresses today. He had something else in mind."

On the way home, Clyde insisted we stop and have a few shots of applejack with him at Dick's bar around the corner from the handbag factory Ray managed. It was where his workers hung out. They knew who we were and wanted to buy us drinks but after an hour of it we said thank you. When we finally got back to the house, Richie went downstairs to bed. I left the light on in the upstairs hall and got the keys to Linda's car and drove downtown to see what had become of Ray. I found his car parked behind an apartment house on Oak Street. He had a secretary named Leah who lived on the second floor. I went up and knocked on her door.

"Yes," she said. "He's here. I'll help you get him downstairs. How's school going?"

She made a pot of coffee and he drank some of that and between the two of us we got him downstairs and into his car. It was an unusually mild night for the end of November. He wanted to put the top down for the drive home. He said the fresh air would do him good. I tried to talk him out of it but gave up when he pointed down the parking lot and said, "You go and get in your girlfriend's fancy little shit box and leave me alone."

I shut my mouth and started across the lot. Before I reached the Ghia, the El Dorado roared into life, shrinking with amazing rapidity down the dark alley adjacent to the building. He took it right through the stop sign and fishtailed out onto Railroad Street. Another tire squeal, and the car disappeared from view. I jumped in the Ghia and followed after him as fast as I could.

I tried to keep up with him, but his taillights kept growing smaller. He must have been doing eighty when he hit the railroad tracks. The car bucked him straight up in the air. His head and shoulders rose above the top of the windshield but he kept his gaze fixed straight ahead and somehow held on to the steering wheel. When he came down, his tailbone landed on top of the seat. Instantly he slid back down behind the wheel and sped up the hill. I didn't try to keep up with him after that. My heart was beating too fast and I felt weak all over at what I'd seen. If he wants to kill himself, I thought, let him get a good head start so I don't have to watch.

I slowed at the cemetery to see if he'd taken the corner all right. The concrete Jesus near the road was still on his pedestal, surrounded by the usual congregation of tombstones. He'd already knocked down it on other wild nights. But this time the fence was still up and no fresh tracks were disturbing the repose of the dead. I began to breathe easier. It looked like we were going to make it home with no more than the usual neurological damage.

When I pulled into the driveway, he was already in the house and all the lights were out. I figured he had gone to bed with his clothes on, as he often did at the end of a rampage. The El Dorado was in the driveway with the top still down but no keys. I thought of going in the house and waking him so I could get his keys and put the top up for him. But I didn't think he would like it if I woke him up. Instead, I lighted a cigarette and thanked God I was going to be out of there in the morning.

It was a nice night. The moon was out, very hard and bright. I got the dogs off the rug in the laundry room and onto their stumpy unreliable legs and took them for a walk around the edge of our property: a nice long walk calculated to make me relaxed enough so I could sleep. The walk did the trick. The fat lazy dogs and I slept together as soundly as the Seven Sleepers of Ephesus until the birds in the trees outside my window (singing in Greek?) woke me the next morning and I got out of there.

CHAPTER | THREE

I had been waiting a long time for my life to begin, and now as I sped across the Verrazano Narrows Bridge in Linda's sporty little car and pointed it in the direction of the Southern State Parkway, it seemed to me that it had begun. The window was partly cranked down. The intoxicating currents of coppery autumn air told me so in exhilarating little slaps to my face as I aimed the car for Bergen Cove where Linda and her family lived. I thought the Gaglianos would turn out to be at least a gateway drug to the life I had in mind. I was a foolish boy, with a bird's fascination for the snake that was about to eat him.

I hadn't asked Linda if the stories Arthur told me were true. I figured she would deny it. There was no advantage in telling me, or anybody, the truth, whatever that was, and probably it was a lot less lurid than the stuff peppering the gullible (count me in) on campus. But one day she opened up to me about a girl in one of her classes, a squinty-eyed platinum blonde whose skin was the same colorless color as her hair, who with a sweetly poisonous smile had slyly suggested that Linda, with her nice clothes and car and lots of spending money (supplied by surreptitious visits from an old foreign-looking man in a limousine) must be a Mafia princess, without actually daring to come out and say it.

"See?" she said under a lowered brow. "If you're Italian, people think you're in the Mafia! News flash: the Mafia doesn't exist! All you Protestant Catholic haters made it up! It really pisses me off! If you're Italian with money everybody thinks you're a crook!"

"Not everybody," I lied. "I don't think you're a crook."

"I don't even know that girl's name."

She narrowed her eyes and looked at me.

"I really gotta find out her name."

I felt a chill run down my back and thought of Bigelow's broken body lying in the hospital and his frightened parents packing up his room, everybody hot-footing it out of town. Maybe she was thinking about a job for those guys at the restaurant. I confess I wasn't troubled particularly by the idea. Anything was better than the crushing boredom I had felt before Linda entered my life. I had romantic ideas about Italians. They were hot-blooded and warm-hearted, so different from my New England family, who were as cold as the weather they had been born into. I expected the Italians to thaw me out. I didn't realize that my ideas about them were as racist-tinged as the rumors flying around school about Linda and her father.

Linda told me that Fillipo Brunelleschi Gagliano had arrived in this country with three dollars in his pocket. He was an orphan. His mother had died in childbirth; his father, the town goldsmith, had been shot to death by government troops in the doorway of their house in Calitri, a town in the mountains above Naples. Fillipo, ten years old at the time, had been grazed by one of the fragments of the bullets that had killed his father. At eighteen years old, he landed on Ellis Island. After being certified and deloused, he was set free to make his fortune in America. He worked in a cousin's barbershop at two bits a shave and fifty cents for a hair cut. His wife, who was also from Calitri (although he hadn't known her back home), worked in a dress factory. They scrimped and saved until Phil could open his own barbershop. Then they scrimped and saved some more until they had enough for Mrs. Gagliano to open her restaurant, now famous and greatly expanded. After that, they were on their way.

"Mama was the money maker at first," she said. "Now Daddy makes all the money."

She said he owned a string of barbershops, wholesale businesses dealing in personal care products and hotel and restaurant supplies, rental property along Sunrise Highway in Queens and Nassau County, several thousand acres of farmland in Suffolk, stocks and bonds, and other forms of plunder beyond my ability to take in or calculate. All of this had been accomplished by a man who could barely write his name, and never read anything more complicated than the *Daily News*. His was the quintessential American success story.

Of course, this tale of dogged hard work and eventual success secretly disappointed me. I was persuaded that she was protecting him, that he would turn out to be a Mafia don: someone with the cruel swagger of an Al Capone, or wrapped in the sinister silences of a Lucky Luciano, spiraled with blue cigarette smoke, as he sat behind an elegant desk and meted out life and death.

What I got, when I drove through the gates onto the gravel of the gated courtyard in front of their long rambling pale yellow house, was a crook all right, a little bandy-legged old man with a limp, clad in a Mets warm up jacket and a pair of baggy sweat pants with a scant horseshoe of gray hair running from one jug ear to the other; a man with a pitted face who showed me all his teeth at once like a crocodile as he approached the car on sore feet and fumbled with the door handle.

Plagued by arthritis and emphysema, Phil was no Luciano, but he was rather wonderful looking in a ferocious way, with his somber high cheekbones and hooded eyes. He reminded me of a picture I'd seen of Geronimo, the Apache Indian chief. When he smiled at me, it gave his face an expression of voracious appetite, or of sudden excruciating pain, rather than warmth or pleasure. I thought I'd run over his foot. As he clawed my door and showed me all those teeth, I must have started back in alarm, because I heard him growl, "Get outta dere!"

I opened the door. He thrust a stiffened claw at me.

"Hallo! I'm Linda's fahdah. You must be Ur."

Just then Linda flew out of the house with a squeal and threw herself into my arms. She was followed by a big burly guy about

Richie's age, with a massive head and the dark expressive eyes of an operatic tenor. When he was sure she was through squealing over me, he stepped in and gave me his big paw.

"I'm Mario, Linda's brother. Hey nice to meetcha."

I liked him right away. He had even white teeth and a perspirey awkwardness around strangers that put me at ease, since I usually reacted the same way. When I had pulled in, Cousin Vito, in his usual crow black shirt and white suspenders, was polishing the limousine parked under a cluster of convoluted trees that overhung the gravel of the courtyard. Slowly during the greetings and introductions he had inched forward until he hovered over the knob of Phil's bony shoulder. A ghastly smile full of pointy yellow teeth suddenly raised the withered curtains of his cheeks. I nodded my head in acknowledgment; he nodded in return. From the floor of the passenger side I extracted the pea-green gym bag that held my toothbrush and a change of ragged underwear. I put my arm around Linda and we started for the house. As we ascended the steps, I noticed a man with a shaved head sitting at a table under the trees against the far wall of the compound. A checkerboard and a bottle of colorless liquid sat on the table beside him. As his eyes met mine, he saluted me with his glass.

"Who's that?"

"Gino? That's Gino. Hi, Gino!" she waved prettily at him and he waved his glass at her while keeping his eyes on me. Although he was smiling, sneering might be the better word.

"He's Cousin Vito's nephew from Sicily. He's over here helping out for a couple of months. Daddy says he's a good mechanic."

"A good mechanic? Your father needs a mechanic?"

"Yeah, to keep the car running. Cousin Vito isn't up to it anymore."

"I think I've seen him before."

"Yeah? I don't see how. He's only been in this country, like, two weeks."

Except for the bullet head in the courtyard, these people seemed so ordinary that I was somehow both disappointed and relieved. At dinner that night, I met Linda's mother. A small doe-eyed woman with gray hair and a timid smile, she said very little, although I thought I detected an ally in the encouraging looks she gave me. She excused herself early and retired to her room to lie down. She had not been feeling well for some time, Linda said. The doctors could tell them nothing, and the family was very worried about her.

Mario and Cousin Vito had prepared the main dish, a duck and sausage pasta concoction that was delicious. Both had worked in the restaurant kitchen in their time and they were the regular cooks of the household, although Anna, the housekeeper, officially claimed the title. They did let her serve the meal. She was a fat hairy shifty-eyed woman, with a low husky laugh, and when she set the steaming platters and tureens on the table, her big arms trembled, as if with passion.

During dinner, Mario told me that he was "vice president of Pop's company," but it was clear to me even then, that like Cousin Vito, he did whatever Phil told him to do. He fiddled shyly with his wineglass, his balding forehead damp with perspiration, his flushed baby cheeks peppered with a permanent five-o'clock shadow. His sports shirt was open at the throat. Amid the sinuous glint of the woven gold chains around his neck, I could see thick burls of hair attached to his chest like upholstery buttons. As if to reassure me that I was making a good impression on everybody, he smiled frequently and pleasantly at me throughout the meal, with teeth as dazzling white as coconut meat.

Phil had experienced a hot flash as he approached the table and had immediately divested himself of his string tie and heavy blue corduroy shirt. Throughout the meal he leaned on his elbows at the head of the table in his ribbed undershirt, sipped a little wine, and puffed rapidly on an endless string of smelly crooked black cigars. He told me that twice a year he sent Cousin Vito into the city to buy them by the case at the only place that imported them from Italy.

"Nuthin' tastes good to me no more," he rumbled as he waved

away various offerings of food. The others around the table received this information in silence and bent over their plates of duck and pasta, the platters of cut bread, the three carafes of Chianti gleaming like giant black pearls against the long white tablecloth. I learned that this was a formula he pronounced at every meal, much like a surly benediction. Other than that, he had little else to say. He seemed to be a man of few words and long rhetorical silences. But I noticed his yellow eyes suddenly sharpened to cunning pinpoints of light whenever Linda said anything. Plainly she was his favorite child.

Over the fruit and cheese, he said he had noticed the blemishes on my face and told me to cut out the milk and cheese.

"Daddy! You're embarrassing him!"

"Whaddya mean? I'm only trying to help whatsis here."

"It's *Earl,* Daddy."

"I know what it is. Whaddayoo embarrassed, Ur? I don't mean to embarrass you."

"No sir."

"Good. See? He ain't embarrassed."

After dinner, he put his arm around me and said he wanted to show me his study. It was very nice: paneled in dark wood and furnished with chairs and ottomans in burgundy leather and outlined with brass upholstery tacks. He insisted that I sit down and have a little glass of brandy with him.

"Linda tells me you gonna be a pot."

"A poet, yes. Well--I hope so."

A complicitous cackle escaped from his lips, even as he raised a claw as if to repress it.

"They starve to death, eh? How you gonna eat?"

"I was thinking of teaching school."

"Oh. *Un professore.* Well, I wish you much luck with your life. You're a nice boy."

The idea of teaching was new to me, but now that I'd said it, it sounded good. I thought I saw a new gleam of respect light up the corners of his yellow eyes.

"Linda: she likes you a lot, I can see."

"Thank you, sir. I like her a lot too."

He puffed on his cigar rapidly and narrowed his eyes as he studied me.

"Next week we go to Florida for a month. Me, Cousin Vito, Mario: everybody. I got a house down there in Pompano Beach. Right on da canal. Speedboat. Swimming pool. Everything. Why don't you kids come down for Christmas, eh?"

When I hesitated he said, "Don't worry about money. I know it's tough for you college kids. I'll send you the tickets."

"Gee, I don't know what to say, except thank you, sir."

"Forget it. You come down. It'll make Linda happy. I like to see my lil' girl happy. Just like you, eh?"

He showed me his teeth again in that crocodile smile of his and made another growling noise, which I took for laughter, and then he stood up and relieved me of my empty brandy snifter. I gathered the interview was over.

When we came out, Linda took me aside and whispered, "I think he likes you."

"Did you say anything to him about Christmas?"

"Maybe I put a little bug in his ear. Why? What did he say?"

"He said he'd send me tickets so I could come down and spend the holidays with you."

"Oh, that's wonderful! We'll have such a good time."

"Boy, you get whatever you want, don't you?"

"Yep." She batted her eyes at me. "I'm my daddy's little girl. He buys me whatever I want."

At the time, I didn't realize that included boyfriends.

That night we went out to see a movie mentioned in Linda's General Lit class. It was playing in the little run-down theater in town. It was a French film, with subtitles, called *He Who Must Die,* and it was touchingly beautiful. We were practically the only ones in the place. As soon as the theater darkened, Phil, Mario, and Cousin Vito fell asleep instantly, as if under post-hypnotic suggestion. Only Gino stayed awake. Throughout the movie, I could feel his eyes boring into the back of my head.

"Look at those guys," Linda said affectionately. "They don't care about the movie. They'd rather be at the track. They only came because they knew I wanted to see it. I really love those jerks. They'd do anything for me."

Even then, in our early days together, I didn't think she was exaggerating. I remember my throat constricted at the thought that maybe I was in over my head. While they slept (and Gino remained on sentry duty), she and I held hands, munched popcorn, and watched a bunch of Turks and Greeks blunder into a reenactment of the Passion of Christ.

"How can you stand that boring stuff?" asked Mario afterwards. We were outside the theater waiting for Gino and Cousin Vito to bring the car around.

Linda smirked. "Who do you like? Bugs Bunny?"

"At least he's funny."

Phil gave a bone-cracking yawn and scratched his whiskers. He had the collar of his vicuña overcoat turned up against the raw weather, as he opened the door of his limousine and handed Linda into the backseat.

"S'okay," he growled behind his collar. "She got brains. Not like you, stoo-pid."

"What are *you* talking about?" said Mario affably. "You fell asleep too."

The next morning after breakfast (at which Phil limited himself to a cup of coffee and a fragment of anisette toast, coupled again with the announcement, "Nuthin' tastes good to me no more"), Linda and I followed the path around the swimming pool and cabana and down past the converted toolshed where Cousin Vito lived in Spartan simplicity, unlocked the steel door at the bottom of the barren garden, and walked along the beach on the private cove which formed the rear boundary of Phil's property.

The house was modeled after the villas that Phil had seen in the mountains above Naples when he was a boy. It was enclosed by a seven-foot high stuccoed wall with broken bottle glass on top, and it was the same ochre color as the house. In the garden there was a grape arbor, a fish pond, beautiful trees and flowering shrubs of all kinds. At the back of the house he had built a sort of watchtower so his wife could gaze out onto the bay. It had a 360 degree view of the surroundings, but for the brief time I knew Mrs. Gagliano, she was too ill to go up there even though Phil had an elevator chair installed on the stairs for her. The men who were always hanging around the place lugged a table up there and used it as a place to play cards.

We walked the length of the white sand beach, which was closed off by the same kind of walls as were around the house. They funneled down to the dock and boathouse where Phil kept his speedboat. The boathouse was another place where some of Phil's friends hung out. I saw them take the boat out fishing a couple of times, but mostly they sat in lawn chairs on the dock and smoked cigars and watched bird life through binoculars. They were the most ardent birders I've ever encountered. Otherwise, they seemed to have a lot of time on their hands and nothing to do with it. Why Phil let them hang around I can't say. He seemed to like having a lot of people loitering around the house.

Linda and I held hands and threw stones at the sandpipers and gulls. She was a lithe, slender girl in those days with curly black hair and a round baby face and gravely serious brown eyes above a red pouty mouth. She moved on long legs with the sullen grace of a moody ballerina. She twitched and tossed her glossy pony-tail much in the proud and temperamental way that Ray's horses tossed their manes and switched their tails when we let them out to pasture. When she bestowed one of her dazzling smiles on me, it seemed a rare and priceless treasure.

I thought I was in love, because most of the time when I was with her I felt miserable. I carried my lust around with me like grief. It weighed me down and made me ache for release. I dragged it with me everywhere as if in the grip of a low-grade fever that never got any worse and never got any better. I tried the obvious solution one night by slipping my hand up her leg, but she punched my nose so hard (again!) that for a week afterwards I blew bloody gouts into my handkerchief.

I tried to carry my burden with dignity. But it preoccupied me so much and made me so unhappy that often when I was with her I couldn't think of anything to say. That's the way it was that morning as we walked on the beach and tossed pebbles at the birds. She seemed to accept these silences of mine as behavior one would expect from a poet.

Before we left, Phil wanted to show me his in-home barbershop. It was a small well-lighted interior room with a big mirror over a counter under which was a line of cabinets facing a barber chair. There were a couple of side chairs with chrome arm rests, some potted plants, and two framed pictures facing each other on opposite walls, the first a print of Leonardo's "Last Supper," and the other, a picture of some dogs playing poker.

"You like?"

"Yes, it's very nice."

"Sit down. I'll give you a shave."

"Thanks, but I--"

"Sit!"

So I sat. He wrapped my neck with Sanex paper and buttoned me into a barber's cape striped like old-fashioned mattress ticking. He lowered the chair until I was almost parallel to the floor. It was like being on a slab at the morgue. He extracted some hot lather from a machine on the counter and used a brush to lather my face. When he started stropping his straight razor, I remembered how arthritic his hands were and I got scared he might cut my throat by accident. I fought the feeling by closing my eyes and breathing deeply. Arthur had said that Linda's father was known as "Phil the Barber," because (duh!) Phil was a *real* barber. I began to relax. I listened to the insidious rasp of the razor on my barely existent stubble as Phil, pinching my nose one way and then the other, shaved my upper lip. With a forefinger that felt like wood, he tipped my chin back and began to shave my throat, wiping the blade clean deliberately and slowly on the cape by my ear as he told me how important he regarded family.

"Family is everything, eh? You *capiche*? How you call it? Loyal. Everybody is loyal. That's a good thing. You agree?"

"I do. I *capiche*."

He released a lever on the side of the chair springing me upright and held a mirror to my face. He grinned, exposing a horseshoe of pegged teeth in his bottom jaw that somehow reminded me of the whale that swallowed Jonah. Or maybe the one that got Captain Ahab.

"Look!" he growled. "See how pretty you are?"

The face in the mirror didn't look "pretty" to me. It looked terrified.

Despite the irresistible offer of free tickets, I did not spend the holidays in Florida with the Gaglianos. Because on December 17, 1977, my brother Richie took a DC-3, loaded with contraband parakeets and several bales of marijuana, into the side of a remote mountain in Mexico and canceled Christmas for all time.

CHAPTER | FOUR

"**Y**our brother was a wonderful young man."

"He was running dope, Ma. That's what got him killed."

"How can you say that! That's not so! Nobody ever said that!"

"Yes they did, Ma. They told us that when Dad and I went down to claim the body. You know that, Ma. The plane was full of the stuff. Illegal parakeets too."

"Well, I'm sure he didn't know what he was carrying. He flew the plane wherever they told him to."

"Right. He had no idea."

There would be a time and a place for lying about him, but for a short time among ourselves we would admit the truth about him before we surrendered it in the face of sympathetic friends and nosy relatives: our idol had fallen out of the sky and smashed to pieces on the hard basalt of an ancient mountain. Had he been caught before takeoff at the airport in Oaxaca, he would have spent the next twenty years in a sewer the Mexicans were pleased to call a jail. Given a choice, he would have gone for the mountain. So let us recite his true history before we lose it in a thicket of lies.

He was his mother's darling. In high school, he played football in the fall, basketball in the winter, and baseball in the spring-all with consummate skill and grace. Nola went to all the games in the enthusiastic clubby company of the mothers of the other players. Richie was always the best player on the team no matter what the sport. Those four years were the happiest of Nola's life. She was pretty much off the booze and kept the pills to a minimum. She didn't need that stuff; she had her young Apollo to worship.

She kept a scrapbook of his accomplishments. He was often in the papers. In his senior year, he was voted the best basketball player in the conference, although he was only five feet nine. He played four years of varsity football and baseball and was selected all-county in each sport several times. It took five bulging scrapbooks to hold the accounts of his achievements.

He was an indifferent scholar, seeing no point to it, since his destiny lay in professional sports. Nola was sure that if she hadn't gone to the principal and complained about Miss Sullivan, he wouldn't have passed senior English. She was a difficult old maid who'd been around longer than the building. She had it in for him because he was a gridiron hero with an obvious contempt for Shakespeare. He would walk around the house declaiming in a silly voice, "Me thought I heard a voice cry, 'Miss Sullivan is a shithead!'"

"You know how jealous people like that can be."

I said I certainly did.

No doubt better grades would have brought more scholarship offers than he got. People like that old maid tried to hold him back. Then there was his size. College coaches held a grudge against little people. As it was, he was still able to choose among some respectable offers from several small schools. He took what looked like the best and picked an obscure college in southeastern Missouri. She didn't understand why he had to choose one that was so ungodly far away.

"It's the boy's life," said Ray. "Let him go where he wants."

"You!" she shot back venomously. "What do you care where he goes! I never saw a father like you!"

Unfortunately, things didn't work out in Missouri. He couldn't see to throw the football over his linemen. They were much bigger than the ones he'd operated behind in high school. But he learned to drop back fast and spot his receivers almost by instinct.

The real difficulty was the coach; he was unhappy no matter what Richie did. He simply wanted a bigger kid for the job. He had his eye on a big strapping farm boy who was planning to transfer from a small school in Georgia if the details could be worked out.

Richie had never figured as second string in any coach's plans before. It didn't fire him up, as it might have some athletes. Instead it affected his self-confidence. Secretly he had always suspected that his athletic ability was a kind of magical trick that he might lose the knack of conjuring at any minute. That was what seemed to be happening to him now. He told me this one night over the telephone.

"Cheer up and do your best," I said.

"What the hell would you know about it?"

He was right. I didn't know anything about the special problems of athletes, who die twice, not like the rest us: once, when their otherworldly skills decay and leave them bereft of purpose; and a second natural death, after a tormenting allotment of years as a has-been.

He suffered a shoulder separation in the third game of his freshman season, just as Nola and Ray were preparing to fly to Missouri and see him play the following weekend. The injury finished him for the year. Early the following season, playing in the last quarter of a runaway game as backup for the new boy from Georgia, he injured a knee, and that finished it. Soon afterwards he dropped out of school.

Ray gladly would have paid to have him finish his education. He made that plain during the series of long desperate telephone calls that Richie made home in the aftermath of his injury. Nola and I listened in on the extensions. We offered up driblets of commiseration and encouragement. But only Ray gave him any useful advice.

"Stay in school. I'll pay for it. So you won't be able to play football. Big deal. You'll live. Who knows? You may even thrive."

But Richie said it was too embarrassing, now that he'd lost the scholarship.

"I thought the idea was to get an education," said Ray.

Richie agreed that that was probably the idea for normal people, but he didn't feel normal.

"I'll send you to another school. Under an assumed name, if it'll make you feel better."

Richie thanked him and said he'd think about it. The next thing we knew, he'd dropped out of school. Too mortified to return home and explain his failure to hometown fans and friends who had expected big things of him, he decided to stay down South. He qualified for a commercial pilot's license and got his job flying freight out of Tampa.

It broke Nola's heart when he decided to stay down South. She regarded the Mason-Dixon Line as the entrance to the Underworld. She couldn't imagine anyone passing through it willingly. She related her grievances in a long candid letter. After several weeks, he responded with a postcard, addressed to us all, which had a picture of a pelican on it and a one word message: "Happy."

"Happy! How could anyone be happy in a hellhole like Tampa! I bet some girl down there is wrapped around him like a snake."

Then she lost him completely, suddenly and forever. Not to some picture of Hell she had in her mind about Tampa, a place she had never been, or to some serpent woman with diabolical powers, but to a mountain in Mexico. She could understand the dangers she had named as a magical way of protecting him, but she had never considered mountains, or the mechanical failure of airplanes or, possibly, that her beloved son, bereft of his special gifts, would choose to fly into one.

Ray and I arranged to have the body flown by airfreight from Tampa to Portland, Maine, where it was met by Parker Foss, our long time family undertaker, and transported to Dunnocks Head for interment in the Nichol plot at Burr's Cemetery. He would rest, Nola decided, with her parents-between my grandfather, Dillard, who had taught him to play baseball, and my grandmother, Ruth, who had made his childhood glorious by feeding him homemade donuts and angel food cake. Nola wanted him back in Maine in the soil of his forefathers where she said he belonged. She wanted him next to her parents, who had loved and nurtured him when he was a little boy. That left only one space in the plot. Presumably that one was reserved for Nola. Where Ray eventually came to rest was his own affair.

The day we buried Richie she said to me in a sick whisper, "Your brother was the only person who ever understood me. I don't know what I'll do without him."

I said, "You still have me and Dad."

The words must have struck her heart like bullets of ice. No one could possibly fill the void made by the loss of her young Apollo. We were walking toward the car. She was leaning on me heavily. Ray was still by the gravesite, talking with the other mourners, mostly distant cousins, and old great aunts and uncles, solemn and wrinkled as sea turtles.

Nola patted the back of my hand and looked up at me.

"You," she smiled wanly. "You have your own life to live."

I did, and I made quite a mess of it.

CHAPTER | FIVE

When I visited Bergen Cove at Thanksgiving, Phil had told me that he and Mario owned "da leg of a nag," that was scheduled to run at Pimlico at the end of the season. It had been agreed that he and the boys would stop at the college and take Linda and me along to Baltimore on the appointed weekend, the second one in January, right after the start of the spring semester. Mrs. Gagliano was not up to traveling and had no interest in racetracks. She was to remain home under the watchful eye of Anna, the housekeeper.

I had no more interest in seeing Pimlico than Mrs. Gagliano, particularly at that time of the year, even though Phil assured me it was one of the most beautiful racetracks in the country. But I did like the idea of staying at the first class hotel he said he'd have Mario book us into, and of having dinner at Magdalena's, "a joint," he growled in a low suggestive gravelly voice, "that maybe you kids'll like, eh?"

He lazily blinked his yellow eyes at me and punctuated each of these relatively innocuous words by slightly tapping the smoky air above his bald head with the glowing tip of his cigar as he said them, as if they contained much hidden meaning. At the same time he smiled at me, shooting me another glimpse of that astonishingly painful-looking grimace full of peg teeth, before his heavy cheeks, flushed and shiny with wine, collapsed again into his customary deadpan expression. That grim piratical smile signaled complete confidence in my understanding, but the truth is, I had no idea what he meant. Later Mario took me aside to whisper that Magdalena's was an experience I shouldn't miss. That he was fat, and obviously given to the enjoyment of good food, added special authority to his opinions about restaurants.

Richie's death, however, had a sudden calamitous effect on my ideas of what constituted a good time. I was no longer interested in fine food, or free lodging, or in going anywhere with anybody, especially the Gaglianos. I tried to buckle down to my studies, but I couldn't keep my mind on my work. I kept fretting about how Nola and Ray were managing at home without me. I told Linda what was troubling me, and said I wanted to go home and see how they were doing, instead of traipsing off to Baltimore for the weekend. I apologized for ruining everybody's plans. I said I thought I could talk Arthur into giving me a lift. She was disappointed; she thought a trip away would do me some good.

"Can't you go home next weekend?"

"I've got a test I have to study for."

"If you don't want to go with us, I understand."

I didn't think she understood at all. With a growing sense of irritation concerning why any explanation was needed, I tried to keep my patience and explain it to her the way you would to a spoiled three-year old.

"I'm worried about them. I can't go off and have a good time with that on my mind."

A flutter of panic crossed her face.

"You don't mind if I still go with Daddy, do you?"

I assured her that I didn't. I told her to go and have a good time for the both of us, and to be sure to thank her father for inviting me.

"He'll really be sorry that you're not coming with us."

"I'm sure you can explain why."

"I'll try," she said.

It was at this point, when my exasperation was reaching its limits, that she surprised me with one of her sudden acts of generosity. She rummaged in her purse and tossed me the keys to the Ghia.

"Take my car. Then you won't have to beg Arthur for anything. He'll want you to help him with his Chaucer or something. Hey, wait a minute."

She dug further into the jumble of lipstick tubes and chewing gum.

"I can give you some gas money too."

Full of gratitude, I gave her a chaste brotherly kiss on the cheek and told her that she was a wonderful girl, which made her beam with pleasure like a little child. Then, well in advance of Phil's expected arrival, I stole out of the parking lot in Linda's car and drove the forty-five miles to the sooty little town of Aldridge and up the ridge above the town where our house was.

They were sitting in the kitchen over coffee. Nola was in her robe and pajamas, and her hair was standing up on the back of her head where she'd slept on it all afternoon. Ray was in his shirtsleeves and slippers having a cigarette. It looked as if I had walked in on them at a particularly dreary moment. I think they were relieved to see me.

"Why Early," said Nola, sounding pleased. "What are you do-ing home?"

"Hi, Ma."

"Good God," Ray said, grinning. "Look what the cat drug in. I thought you were going to the races."

I noticed the difference in him right away. He looked thin and sick.

"What's for dinner?"

"I thought I'd fix some Chop Suey."

"I can always come back tomorrow."

He laughed.

"You can have a grapefruit with me, if you like. Your mother's got me on this diet she found in the newspaper. I've lost twelve pounds already."

"No wonder you look so bad."

"Are you kidding? I've got forty pounds to go."

"Well, go easy. You don't want to overdo it."

"Your mother's worried too."

He grinned at Nola, who, in her old pajamas and bathrobe, was languidly watching us from her seat at the table in the breakfast nook, nursing a cup of coffee that looked as if it had gone as sour as a sinkful of old dishwater.

"She's afraid I'm liable to get so good looking I'll have to fight off all the women down at the factory."

"You leave those poor women alone! They have enough problems without you disrupting their lives."

"You'd better go slow," I said. "A quick drop in weight isn't good for you."

He pointed his thumb at me and cocked his head at Nola.

"Listen to him. He's been on my back to lose weight for years. Now when I do, he wants me to stop."

They put on a brave front for my benefit that weekend. Even Nola tried her best to stay awake, although she didn't get dressed or ever get around to combing her hair. But she was conscious mostly, and smiled weakly in my direction whenever I entered a room.

On Saturday night we even played a few listless hands of Canasta before we crept off to our beds, relieved to be alone in the dark again, and free of the pretenses we'd kept up for each other's sake. When I was ready to leave for school on Sunday afternoon, Ray walked me out to the car. Looking haggard and a little ludicrous in his baggy slacks, he gave me a determined smile and waved goodbye as I started up the driveway. In the rearview mirror, as I turned into the road, I saw him still waving. His pant cuffs flapped against his ankles as smartly as yacht club pennants snapping in the breeze against their flagpoles.

This image of him, standing in the wind on the edge of the drive, looking thin and haggard, with his pants flapping around his legs, stayed with me down at school. It disturbed me. Sometimes it materialized on the page of Ruskin or Carlyle before me, as I tried to study. It woke me up at nights. Three weeks later, I hitched a ride with Arthur and went home again. Ray had lost another eight pounds and admitted this time that he wasn't feeling right. He had given up the grapefruit diet, which he said was the root cause of his problems.

"It was the damned diet. You couldn't keep a fruit fly alive on it. Your mother comes up with the silliest ideas. I don't know why I let her talk me into these things."

He had gone back to his usual fare: thick slabs of rare roast beef slathered with mushroom sauce, with mashed potatoes and gravy on the side; steaks and fries; beans and hot dogs with the special cabbage salad he had invented, made with lots of sliced-up green olives, carrot shavings, and mayonnaise; the coffee ice cream with walnut topping that he ate in the evenings while sitting on the sofa in front of the TV with Nola. He went back on the booze. But that wasn't working either. He was feeling nauseous all the time and leaving most of his food on his plate. He couldn't finish his drinks. He was still losing weight.

"That fool diet has caused me to lose my appetite. It'll probably take me months to get feeling right again."

He told me he was having trouble sleeping at nights. That was not like him at all. Ordinarily he fell asleep the second his head hit the pillow. Now, when he finally did drift off, he often woke a few minutes later bathed in sweat. He found himself going into the bathroom in the middle of the night to check his temperature with the old thermometer of dubious accuracy that lay in the medicine cabinet among the litter of Nola's extensive pharmacopoeia of nostrums and knockout drops. He seemed to be running a mild fever on and off, although it was hardly noticeable, only two or three degrees above normal. He always woke in a sweat at daybreak, he said. Usually he felt pretty good after that, if a little weak. His temperature was always normal in the mornings.

"I've got some kind of a virus I can't kick. My system's all fouled up. If I could get a good night's sleep-"

"Go see Dr. McSherry," Nola said. "Let him give you a vitamin B-12 shot. That'll fix you up."

"Get one in your ear. I'm not going to that quack."

He finished with his usual spiel about doctors.

"If you got anything more wrong with you than a cold, they have to make it up as they go along. Thanks but no thanks. I don't want to be one their guinea pigs."

"Well then, take one of my sleeping pills, so at least you can sleep at night."

"Last time I took one, I was up on the roof every night for a week, baying at the moon. Don't you remember?"

"Oh, land sakes," Nola pushed away her coffee cup. "You talk some sense into him, Early. He won't listen to me."

McSherry was the dapper little pill pusher who wrote Nola's pep pill prescriptions whenever she called him on the telephone. I liked him, and so did Ray. Sometimes he came up to the house and talked horses with Ray down by the fence. Although Ray liked him personally, he had no use for doctors as a matter of principle. One had vaccinated him with a dirty needle when he was a kid, and he had nearly lost his arm because of it.

"Why don't you go see him, Dad? He knows what you're like. He won't try anything silly on you. He might be able to help."

"God," he sighed. "Don't I love it when you two gang up on me. All right, all right. I'll go see the son of a bitch."

I told him to call me with the results, and two weeks later, he did.

"He put me in the hospital for some tests. I told him I'd give him twenty-four hours, then I was clearing out of there. He said that was okay, that was all the time he needed. So I went in there, and they poked and stuck things in me, took a picture of my chest, and then I went home. They didn't find a thing. He called me into his office a week later, and said my white blood cell count was a little elevated, but other than that, they couldn't find anything wrong with me. He thought maybe it was stress or depression, so he gave me some Librium. By God, I have to say I think it worked. I feel pretty good again."

"Good," I was relieved.

"Say, when are you coming home again? Your mother likes

having you around the place. Particularly, you know, with Richie gone."

Midterms were coming up and Linda was feeling put out and neglected by all my scurrying back and forth, so I hadn't planned on going home for another week. But one night, around three o'clock in the morning, Nola called and changed my mind in a hurry. I could hear the edge of hysteria in her voice.

"You'd better come home. Your father's sick. I can't cope with this alone."

She said she got up in the middle of the night, very careful not to disturb Ray, who was making horrible noises in his sleep in the other bed. She couldn't stand it; she had to get out of there. She was worried sick about him, she said. He was still losing weight and he hadn't been acting right. With Nola, as with all of us, sometimes worrying about somebody makes you aggravated by everything they do. In this case, it was Ray's snoring. She put on her robe in the dark and felt her way out of the room with her hand in front of her, so she wouldn't run into the edge of the door, as she had one night many years before. She'd gotten two black eyes and a big knob in the middle of her forehead that night. Richie and I, she reminded me, had called her "the Mother Raccoon" for weeks afterwards.

Well, she wasn't going to repeat the experience if she could help it, but she didn't want to turn on the light either and disturb Ray, so she felt her way out to the light switch in the hall. She was in the kitchen. She thought it might be nice to have a real cup of coffee instead of instant for a change, like Ray made for her sometimes. As she was standing there, trying to figure out the intricacies of the coffee maker, Ray crept up behind her and gave her the fright of her life. She startled him too, when she jumped and cried out, because he started to swear at her, and said she was "a bloody nervous Nelly," and if she'd sit down and get the hell out his way he'd make the coffee for her. He had an old moth-eaten army blanket slung over his shoulders.

"Why are you dragging that horrible thing around with you?"

"Because I got the chills. Is that all right with you? Now sit down and get out of my way, so I can do this little job."

As he poured the coffee, she wondered in a meek voice if there were any more cookies in the house. He said he would investigate. He found some Toll House cookies that weren't too stale and put some on the tray with the coffee and brought it over to the table.

"He looked so horrible, lugging that tray over to the table, with his shoulders bent and that old blanket hanging off him."

"Get to the point, Ma."

"Shut up and let me talk. It's my nickel."

She was so worried. He looked so awful. She thought she'd better not look at him. But that didn't help. When she bit down on her cookie, she was so nervous that the crunch sounded like a cat biting down on the skull of a mouse. She tried to make pleasant conversation. She told him what good cookies he had found for them.

"I told him they were almost as good as Mother's. You know what he said? He said, 'Your mother's been dead for fifteen years'! That's all he could find to say by way of an answer to my attempted pleasantry. I knew he was feeling miserable. He always talks that way when he's feeling really bad. He gets like a bear with a sore backside. Then I noticed he was just sitting there. Sitting there. Looking at his coffee cup. He hadn't even taken one sip. I said, 'What's wrong, Boggy?'

"Oh, Early! He looked up at me, so sweet, with a little smile on his lips, and he said, 'I don't think I can lift it up.'

"It nearly broke my heart when he said that. When I think what a strong man your father always was! I went over to his end of the banquette and told him to scooch over and I held the cup to his lips and he took a sip. 'There,' I said, 'isn't that nice? Have a little bite of cookie.' His eyes were closed. Tears were running down his cheeks. I don't think I ever saw your father cry before. Only he wasn't exactly crying; he was so exhausted, by the effort of sitting there upright in the booth with me and taking that little bit of cookie.

"'God,' he said to me in a whisper. 'I could lay my head down on your lap and go to sleep forever.'

"'Don't talk like that!' I said. 'What are you trying to do-scare me witless?' I waited for him to make some smart remark about my wits, but he didn't say anything. I said, 'Would you like to go back to bed now?' and he nodded, and I helped him back to the room and got him untangled from that smelly old blanket, and lifted his feet up under the covers for him. He's so weak, he had to hold on to the wall in the hallway. Oh Early, I'm so afraid! I think he's really sick! Really sick!"

She paused, as if for refutation. I didn't know what to say. Then I heard her whisper, "Oh my God! I don't know what I'll do!"

"Try to get some sleep, Ma. Call McSherry in the morning. Get him in to see him as soon as possible."

"I don't think I can," she whispered. "I'm so worn out by all this. Can't you come home and help me with your father?"

"I'll get a ride. I'll be there sometime tomorrow. Try to get some sleep."

So I went home again and saw for myself that he was a very sick man, although he still blamed it on the grapefruit diet. This time McSherry sent him to Joseph Berger, an internist at the Pressman Clinic in Harrisburg. He was the one who found the tumor on Ray's kidney. When the biopsy report came back and McSherry told him it was cancerous, Ray started downhill fast. He had lost a cousin and an uncle to the disease and had always dreaded it, certain it would catch up to him someday and torture him unmercifully. His "cancer attacks," shooting pains in the rectum, usually brought on by a twelve hour drive to Maine, were another thing Richie and I used to kid him about when we were kids.

"Dad's having another cancer attack," we'd say, and fall together on the backseat, laughing hysterically. It made me wince to remember it now.

He got so bad during the slow painful weeks that he had to endure, while he waited for the test results, and then for Joseph Berger to get him in to see Payne, reputedly the best surgeon around, and then for Payne to schedule him for surgery, that I thought he was going to die before he got any treatment. But following the operation and some chemotherapy, he began to improve.

When he came home from the hospital, he stripped off his shirt and showed me his incision. It was healing beautifully. The doctors told him that he healed with the speed of a young boy, not at all like a fifty-three year old man. He was proud of that. Over the course of several weeks, he showed me the scar many times again and repeated what the doctors had told him about his amazing recuperative powers.

Through all of this he'd steadily lost more weight, until now he was about as skinny as his old wormy Palomino down in the pasture. His face was sunken and drawn, and his clothes hung on him as if draped over a hanger. But he seemed happier, more at peace with himself than I'd ever seen him.

One afternoon, when we were sitting out on the deck, enjoying some mild fragrant early spring breezes together, he cocked his head and, leaning over the arm of his Adirondack chair, fixed me with one of his patented squinty blue-eyed glowers.

"I'll tell you something," he confided. "You wouldn't believe the experiences I had when I was lying sick as I've ever been in your mother's bedroom. The things I saw--unbelievable. I can tell you this. There really is life after death."

I must have looked skeptical, because he narrowed his eyes and stuck out his jaw, as if getting ready to throw a punch if I gave him any back talk.

"You can bank on it, pal. I've been there. I've seen it for myself."

When I didn't try to argue how you're liable to imagine anything when you're sick and delirious, it restored his faith in me, because he sank back in his chair and decided to confide in me some more.

He smiled and said softly, "I saw your brother. He told me to say hello."

Suddenly, I couldn't see. I reached out blindly and gave his poor bony hand a squeeze, and we sat there, saying nothing to each other, holding hands like a couple of girls, and looked out over his pasture and his scraggly horses, to the mountains in the distance.

CHAPTER | SIX

Near the end, they catheterized him and drugged him up and left him pretty much to himself. He had a nice peaceful room on the second floor of the clinic, down at the far end of the hall, out of everybody's way.

Some of the men from the factory came to see him. They sat with their caps on their laps and tried to talk to him, as though he was the same man they'd always known. But when he looked at them and then looked away and didn't answer, their feelings were hurt and they were confused.

I told them not to take it personally. I said, "It's the disease. It's gone to his brain. He can't talk anymore. He doesn't know anybody. I don't think he even knows where he is. But I think he still likes to have company."

Some of them broke down when I told them that and said they weren't coming back. They couldn't stand to see him that way. I said maybe it was best: stay away and remember him the way he used to be. Nola was too sick to go see him. It was probably a good thing. It would have broken her heart and, God knows, he had already done that often enough.

I dropped out of school and took a part-time job in the produce department at the Weis Market. Every night after work I took a sandwich, which the nice Pennsylvania Dutch lady at the deli counter fixed for me, and went over to the hospital and sat with him while I watched the news and ate my dinner. I didn't try holding any one-sided conversations with him. When I was finished with my sandwich and the news, I kissed his forehead, said goodnight, and cleared out of there.

When he got it over with, we took him back to Ligget and buried him next to his mother and father on a hillside overlooking the Kennebec. We got an auctioneer in and sold the house, the horses, the automobiles, and the extra furniture Nola wouldn't need in the new little house that she'd bought for herself and the dogs.

Nola needed the cash. Ray had made good money, but he spent it faster than he could make it. He died without life insurance. He left behind lots of bills, including the mortgage, installment loans on the cars, some financing for part of my college tuition, feed bills for the horses, and lots of hospital and medical expenses his medical insurance didn't cover. Fortunately the house had appreciated considerably. After she paid off everything, Nola had enough left over to buy her new little house, and she put the balance on interest at the bank. It wasn't much, but it would keep her and the dogs in kibbles for a while. Someone at the bank told her she would be eligible to collect reduced social security benefits at age sixty-two.

"I can't wait," she told me. "I wish I could take a pill that would make me age faster."

During all this, Linda was going through her own bad time. Her mother's illness was getting worse; she wondered whether she ought to drop out of school as I had and go home and be of help. Phil didn't think it was necessary and ordered her in his harsh peremptory fashion, which I know hurt her feelings, to quit calling home and attend to her studies.

I made it down to Parkman some weekends, but now that I'd bagged it, I felt out of place and uncomfortable. I suspected, perhaps unfairly, that Arthur and my other so-called friends, made up of a small supercilious circle of English Lit. majors and the theater kids, regarded me as the victim of some horrible bad luck, possibly contagious, and that they really wanted nothing more to do with me. More likely they were simply busy. Parkman is a demanding school. They had already expressed their sympathies, both because my father was sick and because it had forced me to leave school. Certainly that should have been sufficient. But I kept on obtruding my sorrowful face into the middle of their busy schedules when for all intents and purposes everything to do with me should have been finished business.

As Ray's illness dragged on, I went down to school less and less. Linda and I kept in touch by telephone in a sort of half-hearted, desultory fashion. Our conversations were dull and listless. We didn't seem to have much in common except our family miseries, and these were driving us apart rather than together. Over the telephone, we didn't seem quite real or relevant to the other. We were both too numb to care. This was the moment when we could have gone our separate ways, mercifully, with no hard feelings. Except for Phil's intervention, it might well have turned out that way.

Linda never called me. I always had to initiate the calls. I half suspected that she'd taken up with someone else and was waiting for the right moment to break the news to me. If only I'd had the sense to stop calling her, our relationship would have died the natural death that it deserved.

Phil, on the other hand, often telephoned *me*. Sometimes Nola would be out of bed, flapping around the house in her bathrobe and pajamas, and she would answer the ring. Immediately I would know it was him on the line because she would always make a face and cover the mouthpiece and whisper, "It's that horrid old *Italian* man again."

If I was within twenty-five feet, I could hear him shouting through the earpiece in the raspy irascible voice that he reserved for dealing with the exasperations brought on by all forms of modern technology except for the automobile, in which he could merely sit while others drove and did what he told them to do. Had Phil his way, we would still be communicating by drum and signal smoke.

During the dragged out sad times of Ray's terminal illness, my daily rounds consisted in doing the minimum amount of housework around Nola's house and seeing that she got something to eat and took her medication. I let the horses out into the pasture, fed them oats and hay, mucked out their stalls. I also saw to it that the poor old dogs, poofed out in their dull matted snarly coats, were led down the back steps on their spindly legs to effectuate a more or less daily poop in the backyard. That, and sleepwalking through my work among the fruits and vegetables in the produce department at the Weis, and visiting my insensate father in his stuffy room at the Pressman Clinic. Phil's calls cleared my head immediately, like a dose of smelling salts. They were always a welcome break.

"Hallo hallo!" he shouted down the line. "Hallo, hallo, who's dis? I wanna talk to-goddam, what's wrong with dis ting? Hallo hallo!"

I held the phone away from my ear as he began knocking it against something at his end, most likely against the edge of the Moorish stand in the hallway where I'd seen a telephone on my visit to Bergen Cove. He hammered the receiver about like a pipe smoker clearing his briar against a fence post, apparently with some idea of getting it to do his bidding. Usually it took me a minute or two to get him calmed down long enough to realize that he had me on the line.

"Ur! Ur, is that you, eh? Heh, heh."

This was followed by some gratified gurgly growling sounds deep in his throat.

"Hallo, hallooo. How are you, eh? It'sah nice to hear you. I been trying to reach you all week but they keep giving me the wrong numbah."

"Hello, Mr. Gagliano! How are you, sir?"

"Hallo, hallo? What the-Ur, you still somewhere?"

"Yes, sir!"

I always had to shout in return, so he could hear me over his own voice. Satisfied the technology was holding up under the strain of this connection, we would make the appropriate inquiries about the sick, and he would usually end by saying that he hoped I would be able to travel home with Linda to visit them sometime soon; and then he would slam down the receiver, usually while I was still in the middle of thanking him for his call.

This string of telephone calls puzzled me as much as they pleased me. I was glad he cared about me and my problems at a time when no one else seemed to, but I didn't understand why. One night, when he had me summoned to the telephone, he told me that if I needed any money for tuition, or anything else when I started back to school, I should come to him.

"Don't go to da banks. Those thieves. They want blood outta cabbages."

I thanked him. I was flattered. I told him that I thought I would be able to manage all right. This was pure bluff, because I had no money for school and didn't know where to get any. Phil got so mad when I made, what seemed to me, this modest refusal, that for a moment I thought I had Donald Duck on the line.

"Don't insult me when I offer you help! Whaddayou, think it's a disgrace when somebody offers help with your life?"

"I'm sorry. I didn't mean any-"

"Listen to me! Don't insult me like this! You hear me?"

"Yessir, I hear you, Mr. Gagliano."

"Okay. Okay," he sounded somewhat mollified. "I tole ya, call me Phil. Nobody calls me Mr. Gagliano except maybe for a few waiters lookin' for a big tip. Listen: you need it, you take it. Hear me? It's no disgrace. You pay me back whenever you can. Okay?"

"Yessir. Thank you very much."

"Good, good. You're a nice boy. How's you fahdah? Any beddah? Aw, too bad. I'm deeply sorry for your troubles."

Shortly afterwards, at the conclusion of these ritual inquiries, he hung up. I had a sense that all his earlier telephone calls had been preliminary to the point that he'd just made so emphatically: that from now on, if I ever needed any help, he would see to it, and he would take it amiss if I didn't come to him.

I didn't realize it then, I was really too stupid to know what was going on, but Phil had made me his son-in-law long before

Linda and I had any idea of getting married. The old man loved me, probably more than Linda ever did. I was suddenly the unworthy Absalom of his bosom. He had race horses. He believed in bloodlines. Perhaps he wanted me in his family as a maker of children with strong bones, high intelligence, no chronic diseases, beautiful grandchildren who would someday rule his empire and compensate for the inadequate son God had given him. I suppose this talent for-what? Acting on assumptions before anyone else knew what they were? Inventing reality by embodying his schemes with money, equipment, and employees? Whatever you called this ability for knowing what was going to happen before anyone else did, even if he had to invent the outcome himself, was likely the gift that had made him a rich and dangerous man.

Shortly after I got back from Maine, after taking Ray home for burial in his parents' cemetery lot, Phil called again to offer condolences (he'd sent a stupendous wreath to the funeral home in Ligget, by far the largest, which put Nola in a snit: *Why would he do such a thing? He didn't even know Boggy!*), and he asked me if I would mind doing him a favor.

"Missus Gagliano is going in the hospital. They gonna try a lil' surgery. See what they can find. My baby Linda should be here, eh? So she can smile on her mother when she comes outta the ether or whatever. I wonder if you mind driving her home for me?"

"Certainly, sir. I'd be happy to."

Of course Linda was perfectly capable of driving home herself. She had the car. All I had was the use of Nola's secondhand Rambler convertible that I had to park at the far end of parking lots because the transmission was so touchy that sometimes I couldn't get it to go into reverse gear. (Years later, when she got Tito, her cocker spaniel, I would see the two of them flying down the road in the selfsame old rattletrap, only now the blue was faded to a dull gunmetal finish and one of the taillights was usually broken from where Nola had run into various obstructions that had impeded her on her rounds of doctors' offices, pharmacies, and grocery stores. Usually the dog would have his head out the window as the car careened past me, his ears flapping in the breeze like the unbuttoned chin straps of an old-time aviator's helmet. Tito would be straining forward, doing his noble-dog bit, peering straight ahead at the road with the solemn *sangfroid* of a fighter pilot in a power dive.)

I was more than pleased to drive Linda home, if that's what Phil wanted. Besides, it would get me out of Nola's dreary house for a few days, and I think Phil wanted me on hand as his own crisis came on the boil. He growled appreciatively, told me Linda would be expecting my call, and nearly broke my eardrum when he slammed down the receiver. Linda picked me up at the house, but made no move to get out from behind the wheel.

"Your father said I was to drive you home."

"Whatever," she shrugged, and scootched into the passenger seat.

Mrs. Gagliano was a shrewd woman. When she came out from the anesthesia, she wanted to know what time it was. It was twelve-fifteen. She had gone on the table at eleven.

"That didn't take long, did it?" she said quietly and closed her eyes.

She had a tumor the size of a bocce ball on the aorta, just above her stomach. The doctors took one look and closed her like a book. The whole thing had taken under forty-five minutes.

When the family came back into the room that night, after their conference with the doctors, the room was already crowded with flowers and relatives. Mario broke into big operatic sobs at the sight of his mother smiling wanly at him from the pillows.

"Mario-stop, stop," she admonished him weakly.

But Mario lost his grip completely. He prostrated his clumsy body by the side of her bed and twisted her hands and howled at the ceiling. His balding head glistened in the light of the bedside lamp as he hid his face from the sympathetic gaze of the crowd of relatives surrounding the bed like figures in a crèche. Crying so passionately made him sweat freely. His big nose ran like a river.

His sallow face grew shapeless as a reflection in a puddle of water. He had no handkerchief. He wetted the front of himself until I could see his dark nipples and some of the buttons of his chest hair showing through his white shirt. Linda went in the bathroom and got him some toilet paper to cry into. Cousins, aunts, and uncles consolingly crowded near while Mrs. Gagliano, the color of cigar ash, lay sweetly serene under the white sheets and feebly stroked his head.

At last Phil grew exasperated and started swearing at him. "No, no, Phil," I heard Mrs. Gagliano say in a piteous voice. But her hand fell away limply to her chest, as if surrendering Mario to judgment. Phil said something else to him in Italian and actually started to raise his crooked hand as if readying to cuff his cowering head. But he was restrained from going further when a matriarchal figure dressed in black stepped forward, an elderly lady from upstate, whom the others addressed as Aunt Tessie, apparently someone of great standing in the family, who told him solemnly that it was a wicked thing for a father to mistreat a sorrowing child.

The doctors gave Mrs. Gagliano six months, but she got it over with in six weeks. During that time, I practically lived at the house in Bergen Cove, leaving only to drive Linda back to Parkman for her final exams and except for one weekend to see how Nola and the dogs were getting along.

The distractions of my old passion for Linda sharpened painfully under the pressure of living in the same house that awful summer. Everything was falling apart. With everybody suddenly dying around us, we glommed onto each other desperately. I needed a few surrogates to fill in the vacancies in my life. Phil and Mario would probably do nicely in this regard, I thought. My mother couldn't help me. Incompetent even in the smallest matters, she had never been able to help me in any practical sense. As a teller of sad but elucidating stories she was excellent. But I had heard all of the good ones by the time I was twelve. And it seemed to me that I could only go on helping her by putting myself at risk:

by living at home; by doing her shopping for her and seeing that she got her prescriptions filled; by doing the heavy lifting around the place. In this scenario, the benchwarmer son finally comes into his own. But I wanted no part of the role. The time for that was long gone. She would have to learn to take responsibility for herself. She would have to find her own way of dealing with desolation, just as Linda and I were trying to do. Nobody was going to take care of her anymore. Certainly not me. I thought all of these thoughts, and they left me aching with a bad conscience.

On the night of the day of Mrs. Gagliano's funeral, Phil and Mario and Cousin Vito and several of the usual hangers-on drove over to Roosevelt Raceway, where Phil bet two hundred dollars on the Perfecta and won over thirteen thousand dollars. They had invited me to go along, but I chose to stay at home with Linda and Anna. Linda told me she was not upset that her father and the others had gone to the track as usual on the day of her mother's funeral.

"You could have gone if you wanted to," she took my hand and smiled. "But I'm glad you didn't."

She explained that Phil was a proud man. Too proud to make much of a public show of grief over something he couldn't change. He would do his mourning in private. The thing was, the planet would go on wobbling through the darkness, no matter who died. She knew that he loved her mother deeply. Deep, deep down, on some pure harsh indivisible level that didn't show, an old love with no flesh on it, just a bag of bones now, but proud, and needing no words or any gratuitous gestures. He would take refuge in the comfort of his regular habits. He would go to the track. He would place his bets as usual. He would win a few and lose a few. He would light one of his stinking cigars and study his program, and go on with his life as best he knew how.

Mrs. Gagliano was interred in consecrated ground following a baroque funeral mass conducted by Father Palumbo of St. Jude's, the church where she and Phil had been parish members for thirty-five years. Somehow, through some funny business,

Phil managed to fly in some soil from Camposanto Monumentale in Pisa, allegedly brought back from Golgotha in the 14th century. Legend had it that bodies buried in it turned to dust within twenty-four hours. After the service, having been displayed in her finery, Mrs. Gagliano was removed from her rosewood coffin, dressed in a simple shroud, and buried in the equivalent of a cardboard box, so the stolen dirt could work its magic before the worms got to her.

Shortly afterwards, in Father Palumbo's oak-paneled study, I began to take instruction in the Catholic faith. The mumbo jumbo he was selling made even the magic dirt sound sensible. At the end of that summer, before the same altar where Mrs. Gagliano's casket had rested so recently, Linda and I were joined in what Father Palumbo and others were pleased to call "Holy Matrimony."

CHAPTER | SEVEN

Eight hundred people attended our wedding and reception. If I'd had my way, we would have crept off and gotten married by the town clerk. But that wasn't what I'd agreed to, when I signed on with Father Palumbo. Except for poor Mrs. Gagliano, who was truly devout, the rest of the family were fairly nominal Catholics. They took a practical view of the church. It was an important local institution, just as were the schools, the banks, and the local branch of the Sons of Italy. They followed form in matters of baptism, marriage, and burial, and made a point to attend Mass during the major holidays. Phil gave generously to the church. He had a pagan's inherent respect for any supernatural powers that might be operating in the vicinity and that could aid or injure his prosperity. It was only prudent to propitiate these forces regularly with little offerings of tallow and fat. It was no different than dealing with the local pols on zoning matters. I also dimly perceived the wedding was to be a moment of high drama in the lives of the Gagliano clan; in their minds the only proper setting for a performance of this magnitude was St. Jude's, with its churchyard containing Mrs. Gagliano evaporated in her holy dirt. Anywhere else was unthinkable.

Arthur Frankenwood was there as my best man. Leslie Zydorczk, leader of the theater rats at school, drove out from the city that morning to be there, which impressed me, since I had never thought he was much of a friend of mine. He'd already started work at Bergman & Childress as one of their book salesmen. Nola was there too, looking shrunken and out of place, dressed in a strand of pearls that had turned yellow with the years, and a green sateen dress that looked awful on her. An old red fox stole that had once been her mother's was slung around her neck, handy in case she wanted to hang herself by a foxtail before the reception was over. She kept it on during dinner because she said the air-conditioning was giving her a chill. She had on a hat too, a little shiny-green pillbox affair of straw, with a fishnet half-veil. It had been knocked askew on her head by Phil when he introduced her with an expansive flourish of his arms to Cousin Alphonse, an important member of the General Assembly in Albany.

I watched her finicking with her plate of filet and lobster tail from our table on the dais. She was seated right in front of us. I couldn't catch her eye. She kept them lowered as she pushed a baked tomato around on her plate. She was trying to ignore the attentions of a deeply tanned gray-haired man in a red Palm Beach jacket and yellow slacks on her right, who seemed ready to bite her on the neck if she didn't talk to him. Her mouth was tightly pursed against the intrusion of this importunate man. She had on too much rouge, and her face looked powdery and drawn. She hated crowds. She hated strangers, especially noisy friendly strangers-and all of these people were noisy and friendly. She looked miserable. I wanted to thank her with a smile for being on hand, but she never looked up. At one point during dinner Linda leaned over to me, apropos of nothing, and said, "Your mother's quite a character, isn't she?" Those were the kindest words Linda ever said about her.

At first, Nola told me she couldn't come to the wedding because of the dogs. She was afraid of driving the Rambler as far as Long Island. The transmission had begun to act up again on her way home from the cottage that summer. She wasn't feeling particularly well either, she said. That's why she'd decided to come back from Maine before Labor Day: to come home and rest, not to run around the countryside. I understood this perfectly, and told her it was all right if she couldn't make it.

But Phil finally talked her into leaving her animals behind

"with a trusted friend," as he put it. This "friend" was a man named Dr. Perlmutter. When he came to the house he looked like he was wearing gag glasses with a fake nose attached. He had a nervous disposition. Every time I mentioned Phil's name it made him jump. It turned out that he had worked as a vet at some of the tracks where Phil's horses ran. No kennel for Nola's dogs. The doctor was going to stay at her house and babysit her animals. It made her anxious to have a stranger in the house, but Phil assured her that she could trust Dr. Perlmutter. He would feed and bathe her dogs, take them for long walks, and do the housework. He had a sleeping bag that he would set up in the sunroom. He would disturb nothing, improve everything. He was an excellent mechanic and he would tinker with her car and see if he couldn't get it to run better. All of this made her feel flustered but very special. With that settled, Phil dispatched Cousin Vito with the limousine to fetch her to Bergen Cove for the weekend, where he and everybody else treated her like visiting royalty.

I met so many people that weekend it was impossible to keep them straight. At the reception Linda introduced me to a series of Uncle Tonys. "Say hello to my Uncle Tony from Poughkeepsie," she would instruct me, and I would turn on my heel and shake the hand of another Tony. Some of them had on their hats and coats, and were in a hurry to get back to Utica or Kingston or wherever they were from. Usually a dark expressive hand, sparkling with a diamond ring, would withdraw a big cigar with a flourish from the middle of a dark saturnine face. With a glitter of pearly teeth, this new Uncle Tony would pump my arm with enthusiasm. A pair of hot dark eyes with whites the color of cooked onions would examine me appreciatively from head to foot.

"Hallo, kid! Welcome to da family."

A fifteen-piece orchestra dressed in baggy dinner jackets did its best to imitate the sounds of Guy Lombardo and the Royal Canadians. There were two open bars on each side of the room and three bottles of Piper Heidsieck on each table when we sat down to our meal. A murmuration of priests suddenly descended on the reception, led by one of Linda's cousins, a boyish looking redhead, and his friends from the nearby seminary. They wolfed down food and drink as if they hadn't eaten in a week.

"Where's Gino? I thought he'd be shaking down the wait staff by now."

Actually I could see him. He was over by the bandstand, a cigar in one hand and a martini in the other, swaying to the music as the band played, "That's *Amore*."

The men paid to dance with the bride. This was Mario's idea. The one or two priests who tried it got to dance with her for free. I thought it was crude and demeaning, but Linda said it was the custom. I sat at Nola's table and watched Linda twirl across the dance floor with a succession of men while Mario worked the crowd for more business. The gray-haired man in the red Palm Beach jacket had finally given up and Nola was sitting by herself.

"You don't look well. You look like you're running a fever. Are you all right?"

I assured her I was fine.

"Linda and I are going to sneak out the side door in a little while, after I toss her garter to the groomsmen."

"Oh, God, how vulgar. Well, tell me before you go. I don't want to sit here thinking you're still here, and you're not. Will you do that for me?"

"Okay, Ma."

As the party was reaching its crescendo and after the thing with the garter, I slipped over and told her we were leaving.

"Take care of yourself, Early."

"Don't look so tragic, Ma. We're only going to the Poconos. I'll see you in a couple of days."

As I turned, I walked directly into Gino's outstretched arms. He gave me a hug that cracked every vertebra in my spine. "*La famiglia. Sì?*" he whispered in my ear.

"I wouldn't know," I said. "I never had one. Lemme go. I can't breathe."

"*Che?*"

"Okay, okay. *Si*, Gino. *La famiglia.*"

He released me with a grin that looked more gorilla than human.

"That's *Amore,* Gino. Go see if the band has any loose change."

He stood there with that frightening grin on his face; that he didn't understand what I was saying was a good thing. Otherwise he might have stuck a thumb in my eye and popped it into his martini.

Mario and Linda were waiting for me by the side door out in the lobby. He'd brought the car around for us. Through the ballroom door I'd closed behind me, I could hear the bogus band begin to play "Seems Like Old Times," and for a moment the sentimental fruitiness of the saxophones quavering out the melancholy old tune filled me with inexpressible sadness. A sudden sense of utter desolation and loneliness swept through me like a cold wind. In my mind's eye I saw Nola, in her moth-eaten stole and her hat knocked askew, sitting alone at the desecrated table in the ballroom, the melted butter for her half-eaten lobster tail beginning to harden on her plate. I knew it was her emotions I was feeling. I wanted to turn back and tell her not to worry, that she wasn't alone, that everything would be okay. I wanted to tell her I would always be around if she needed me. Mario rumped open the side door. I shook myself mentally like a dog coming in out of the rain. As I followed Linda into the parking lot, he handed me a homburg full of cash.

"Here you go, pal. Maybe packed with all the dough it will fit your pinhead," and we all laughed, I louder than the rest, in that goofy falsetto voice I fall into sometimes when I'm really nervous. It looked like a lot of cash. I tossed the hatful of money into the backseat. We hugged and babbled our goodbyes and then Linda and I folded into her little car and started across the parking lot. It had rained, a brief steamy downpour. The air from the open window felt good. The streetlights lit up the puddles in the parking lot and gave the wet paving a satiny sheen. I watched Mario with affectionate gratitude in the rearview mirror as he stood edged in light from the lobby, holding the door and looking comical in his cutaway coat and dove-gray vest, waving goodbye until we turned onto the road and drove from view.

Over the years, I'd told the story of the lucky hatful of money to various people, as an example of how help usually turns up when you need it most. We were married for five years before Linda told me that Phil had slipped at least half of the money into the hat. I heard my voice tremble when I asked her why they'd deceived me like that.

"Because we needed the help, silly. You were acting like such a jackass. It was the only thing Daddy could think of."

I could feel my face burn with embarrassment. I felt like such a pompous ass. I couldn't understand why I hadn't figured it out on my own, when it was so obvious, now that I knew. The only answer is that subconsciously I'd been in on the deception all along.

Before the money fell into our laps, the plan had been that Linda was going to drop out and get a job and put me through my last year. I would work too, part-time. After I graduated and got a job, then she would finish up.

"We'll be like the Eisenhower brothers," I told her. "We'll put each other through school. Won't that be great?"

"I can think of better ways," she said.

"Keep your father out of it."

"I didn't say anything about him."

But that was before the hatful of money showed up. That night in the Poconos, Linda said I was about the luckiest person she'd ever met.

"Things always seem to fall into place for you. Were you always this lucky? Or have you only been so lucky since you met me?"

"It's something new," I said, solemn as a donkey. "I never used to be this lucky."

What a jerk. But Linda liked me that way. She smiled and gave me a kiss.

"What a lucky little boy," she said.

The mountain of wedding presents we received took care of everything else. We had enough linen and china to furnish a hotel. Phil gave us a suite of walnut bedroom furniture that looked like something left over from the Mussolini era. It been brought over in the same shipment as the dirt from Pisa. Mario gave us the living room furniture and the TV. Somebody I never heard of from the Catskills contributed the dinette set. One of the Uncle Tonys chipped in with a washer and dryer; not to be outdone, another Uncle Tony provided us with a double-door stainless steel refrigerator, which we could never use at the apartment because it wouldn't fit in our kitchen. Phil had one of his trucks and a couple of his boys deliver the relevant loot to our temporary digs at school; the rest of the stuff, including the twenty-eight extra toasters, he stored for us in two bays of his five-car garage for over twelve years, until we finally came to roost in our house in Tally-Ho Ford.

Besides ticking off our loot and counting our money, we attempted to put together our matrimonial erector set that first night in the Poconos. We were tired. It would have been better if we had waited until the next day. But we were eager to get it over with so we could go on and have a normal sex life.

"No, no. It doesn't go *there,* dummy."

"Oops. Sorry. Is this better?"

"Yes, that's fine."

"Are you sure?"

"Will you stop talking? Let's just *do* it! Jesus!"

Then later, a subdued review of the performance.

"You scared me. I thought you were having a convulsion or something when you finally-you know."

"Well I was, sort of."

"Was it any good?"

"It was wonderful. Was it any good for you?"

"It was great. Are you sure it was good for you? You act sort of disappointed."

"Disappointed! Me? What a lot of hooey!"

With time, we improved and had a relatively satisfactory sex life, one that kept my low grade fever in check for many years. It was nothing great, but it was certainly passable.

Even though it wasn't necessary, given our newfound riches, Linda decided to drop out of school. She reasoned that she wouldn't be able to go on after I graduated in the spring, since I'd take a job somewhere. So she figured she might as well quit now and save her father's money. She said the other kids treated her differently now that she was married.

"They're a bunch of stiffs," she said.

School was boring and they were boring, so she decided to pack it in.

"Maybe I'll get a job," she said, but she didn't.

She spent a lot of time on the telephone. She wanted to know how things were going back home. She missed the Island, she said. There was always something doing on the Island. She was fond of the telephone. She had relatives in Ossining, Poughkeepsie, Buffalo, New Paltz, and White Plains. She had plenty of people to call, and she liked to stay in touch. I don't know what the bills ran. Phil had the telephone installed specifically so that she could make her calls, and the bills went directly to him.

At night when I tried to study she paced back and forth, from the kitchen to our bedroom in the back. I put the TV and the record player in our room, but she hated to go in there and close the door and watch TV or play records by herself. She said I always ruined it for her, because whenever she went in there and tried to amuse herself, I inevitably knocked on the door and told her to keep it down. She liked to turn the volume up. She was one of those people who needs a certain amount of noise in her life. It acted as a tonic. It soothed her nerves. Me, I liked everything quiet, or "dead," as she put it. My idea of a good time after I got through studying was to sit down with a book. This didn't go over big with her. Some nights I did my studying at the library, but she didn't like that either. She didn't like being alone in the apartment. She was alone all day and that was enough, she said.

One night at dinner she suggested we go to a movie. *Look Back in Anger* had finally made its way to the local art theater and she wanted to see it.

"Not tonight. I have to study for a test."

"You always have to study for a test. Why don't you try studying to be a human being for a change?"

"I can't go," I said. "Besides, we don't have the money."

"Yes we do. Daddy sent me a check."

"I told you not to ask him for money."

"I didn't. He just sent it."

"Send it back. Tell him to stick his jack where the sun don't shine."

That's when I found out when she really got mad she threw her food like a little kid. She let me have it with her plate of spaghetti. The plate hit my chest and landed in my lap. I got so mad that I nearly hit her. I guess she could see it, because her eyes got big and she cringed away from me. Sometimes I wonder what would have happened to me if I had. Maybe Phil would have sent one of his goons to put me out of my misery. I changed my shirt and pants and got my books and started for the door.

"Where do you think you're going?"

She was sitting at the table smoking a cigarette. She hadn't cleaned up the mess yet. There were splatters of sauce and strings of spaghetti everywhere, as if a little bomb had gone off at the table.

I didn't answer. I kept walking.

She said, "If you go out that door, it shuts behind you forever."

"That's okay with me. Go home to your daddy."

When I got back from the library that night, I expected that either she would be gone, or there would be more trouble. But she ran to the door when I unlocked it and threw her arms around my neck.

"I was so afraid you wouldn't come back."

She sounded so frightened, it made my heart swell with love.

"Sweetheart, I'll never leave you. You're my girl."

"Good," she cooed and cozied down into my neck.

That night we made glorious love. She was so completely recovered from her scare that I couldn't help thinking it was all an act.

We spent the Christmas holidays at Bergen Cove. Nola had been invited to stay with her friends the Wilhides at their farm in Virginia, from the middle of December until after the first of the year, so I didn't have that guilt to deal with. Sad to say, Ray's death had a positive effect on her health. She was much less reliant on medication and more often vertical than I ever remembered. She invited Dr. Permutter to look after the house and dogs again and he agreed to do it with what she thought was puzzling alacrity.

"He almost sounded frightened when I asked him. He kept saying 'Yes, yes, yes,' like that silly woman in *Ulysses*."

"You read that book, Ma?"

"Well, I rummaged around in it to see what you were up to. It was in your room when you were in high school. What a smutty book! You should be ashamed of yourself."

I had to laugh.

"You crack me up, Ma."

While we were at Phil's, Linda asked if I would mind if she stayed on and helped out in the restaurant for a while. She was good at doing the books and keeping the waitresses on their toes.

"They really need me around here. They're lost without Mama. You can take the car back to school if you want. You won't have me around to bother you. You can concentrate on your studies. Maybe get a little writing done, who knows? I'll be able to make some money too. That'll help out. I'll send you what I make. Then I won't feel so worthless."

"You're not worthless."

"I *feel* worthless. What do you say?"

I said if that's what she wanted, it was all right with me.

I'm ashamed to say it was a relief not to have her around. Shortly after I got back to the apartment, I had a card from her telling me that they had gone down to Pompano Beach to open up the house for the winter. She stayed down there until the first of April. I was not upset by this development. I had plenty to do. Now that she was occupied, I could get it done.

When I graduated, she wanted me to take a job with her father.

"He'll make you vice president of the company, like Mario. He'll start you at a good salary."

I was already closer to Phil and his operation than I wanted to be. I liked to delude myself that I wasn't in his back pocket. I was his son-in-law, okay. But that was it; nothing more.

"Sorry. I'm not working for your father."

"Will you at least get a job on the Island, please?"

"I'll look into it."

"Daddy will help. The principal at the new high school Daddy built is a friend of ours. Mr. Bleeder. He was at the wedding. Remember?"

That expression "a friend of ours," was like ice water poured down my neck. Phil talked to the man. No surprise, I got the job. Linda was delighted.

"Did he say, 'Yes, yes, yes!' like Dr. Perlmutter?"

"What?"

"It's a joke, Linda."

"I don't get your jokes. They're not funny."

So we moved to Long Island. We rented an apartment in Robinwood, two towns away from Bergen Cove. She was only a few miles from home and that suited her just fine. I taught five sections of freshman English. I liked the kids and had a pretty good time. When I wasn't at school or correcting papers, I worked on my novel. It began as a journal, which I had started when Ray got sick. Gradually it took on a shape of its own, and I thought maybe it would turn into a real book. I worked on it whenever I could, for five years. I used weekends, holidays, vacations, whatever time I could find. I was either working on it, or thinking about it, or loathing the idea of it, every spare minute I had. I read a lot of fiction, hoping I could figure out how to do it by osmosis. Linda had a tough time understanding how I could still be at work when I was reading a book. She spent a lot of time over at her father's house so I could "be alone," as she put it.

I threw away twenty pages for every one I kept. I could hardly stand to read the stuff, it was so bad. It filled me with self-loathing. More than once, after reading a chapter, I went in the bathroom and chucked my cookies. Writing wasn't much fun. I began to think that I didn't have a talent for it. The idea put me in a real sweat. I had no idea what I was going to do if I didn't turn out to be a literary genius. I wrote like a man driving a car with the gas pedal pressed to the floor while pulling on the emergency brake. Everything I wrote I worried to death. I read it over and over again and tinkered with it until I couldn't stand it.

Finally, after years of this, more out of exhaustion than conviction, I got together a slender little smudged-over manuscript of thinly disguised autobiography and sent it off to Leslie, who was by that time an associate editor at Bergman & Childress. I expected to get it back in a month or three, with a polite note attached. But he stunned me by calling one night three weeks later. He said he liked a lot of what I'd done. "You're very talented," he said. I remembered he was theatrical, so I didn't believe him. He said if I were willing to rewrite the middle section, he'd try to work with me. He couldn't make any promises. But if I could fix it up to his satisfaction, he would take it to the editorial committee.

I said I thought I could do that. I held myself in until I got off the telephone. Then I beat the walls, and crowed like a rooster. I tried to call Linda over at Phil's, but no answer. They'd gone out to dinner somewhere. I got out my copy of the manuscript for company and put it on the coffee table, and sat down and had a couple of drinks, and stared at it. The manuscript made a nice neat little block of white paper sitting there on the table. I didn't dare pick it up or read any of it, for fear of ruining everything. I went in the bathroom and talked to myself in the mirror.

"You poor bastard. Maybe you're not a dud after all."

I worked on it for another year. Leslie and I swapped chapters back and forth through the mail and sometimes we talked on the telephone. He was always very cautious. "I don't want to mislead you," he would say. "I don't want to give you any false hope."

Oh no, I said. I didn't feel misled. My hopes weren't up. He felt obliged to say something like that every time we talked. A couple of times, if he'd been in the room with me, I'd have probably killed him. Sometimes I felt I might actually get published. Other times I knew for a certainty that I'd never make it. But finally, one day, he called me up and said they were going to do it.

I suppose I would have gotten more excited if I hadn't been so worn out by all the work that had gone into it. I was happy, of course, but not as excited as I thought I'd be. Leslie had worked all the fun out of it for me. He had to do that. It was an amateur manuscript before he took me in hand. But it wore me out. Still, I thought it might change my life when it was published. Maybe it would sell a million. I thought that would be nice for a start.

When I told her the news, Linda wanted to celebrate.

"Let's go to Bermuda. You deserve a break. You've worked so hard, baby."

We had this conversation by telephone, and I could feel Phil hovering and cackling and rubbing his palms together somewhere in the background. It made me uncomfortable to discuss it over the telephone, but I told her the usual: we didn't have the money.

"Don't be silly. Daddy's so happy for you. You should see him. He's acting like such a nut. He wants us to go. He says after all the hard work, you deserve it. What should I tell him?"

I was too tired to argue. If he wanted to pay, okay. I didn't think I'd taken much from him over the years, although it was a lot more than I was willing to admit, or even knew about at the time. I thought it wouldn't hurt if I caved in this once.

So we went to Bermuda on Phil's money, and stayed at a ritzy little hotel that Linda found advertised in *The New Yorker.* We slept every morning until noon. We sunned ourselves by the pool in the afternoons. We dined in every fancy restaurant we could find. We danced every night in the lounge downstairs at the hotel.

We got tan and sleek, and languid as cats.

When we got back, we found out she was pregnant. We were both a little surprised. She was supposed to be on the pill, but she'd always been a little careless about it. She had the packs with the dummies but she forgot to take them from time to time. Anyway we were surprised, and I, for one, wasn't particularly pleased. I don't think she was, either. But Phil thought it was wonderful. He'd been after us for years to have kids.

When the book came out, hardly anybody noticed. It got a handful of reviews, most of them favorable. The *Saturday Review* liked it quite a lot, calling it "an impressive debut." But the *Times* didn't like it. The reviewer said the book was written by, "an American Camus wannabe" and the smart thing would have been for me to put it in the bottom drawer of my desk. It sold about three hundred copies and was quickly remaindered.

After the book died its quick horrible little death, I had a collapse of my own at work. Everything began to irritate me about the school. I was tired of the chicken shit and the lousy pay. But mainly I was disappointed that the book I'd worked on for so long and so hard, hadn't made a bit of difference in my life. Leslie told me not to be discouraged.

"Write another one," he said.

I didn't think I had another one in me. I didn't want to go through it again. Besides, I thought I'd used it all up. I felt like a kid with a good fastball, who ruins his arm throwing in double A. *Well, you tried,* I thought. At the moment, the long vista yawning in front of me looked pretty empty.

While I was going through the throes of death, life, and publication, my old roomie, Arthur, had toddled off to law school, and then into partnership with his father. His father had a management consulting firm in Harrisburg, called Frankenwood & Son. Only the "son" in this case was Arthur's father, who, in turn, had gone into the business with *his* father right out of the Wharton School.

When he called me up and said they were looking for a writer, I jumped at the chance. He offered me fifty percent more than I was making as a teacher. I felt I couldn't turn it down. I was ready to latch onto a new life. I said to myself: Even if you're not the writer you thought you were, at least you can make some money.

Linda wasn't happy about moving to Pennsylvania. She said if she could have a new car to drive back and forth to the Island, she'd go along with it. We were still driving the Ghia. Phil had wanted to replace it for years, but I'd held him off. Now she saw a way of getting a new car out of the horror of having to relocate to the edge of the known world.

Phil handled it diplomatically. He knew it was a sensitive issue. Mario had a Delta 88 Olds he'd only had for eighteen months; suddenly he developed an aversion for it. He made us a ridiculous deal one night at dinner, which we couldn't turn down. That's the way they got around that one, so little Early's pride wouldn't be hurt. Olds: they don't even *make* that car anymore.

The three of us stayed with Nola until we could find a place of our own. It was only for a few weeks, but long enough for my wife and mother to become undying enemies. The baby nearly drove Nola crazy. It was a small house, and the baby was colicky. She woke up every time the baby did. Which surprised me, because she used to be able to sleep through anything, including Ray teeing off golf balls in the living room. She told me my wife was lazy. When I was gone, she said, Linda let the baby lie in its crib and cry too long before she attended to it.

"She leaves his dirty diapers soaking in the toilet," she said.

This was true. I'd seen this for myself. I thought it was a filthy habit. In turn, Linda told me that Nola was a weird old bitch. She said she couldn't wait to get out of there.

Keefer was born the same month the book came out. He was a much bigger success. She'd had a tough time with him, in and out of the hospital two or three times. When the pregnancy started to get complicated, she moved in with her father, so Anna could look after her. It really looked like we were going to lose him a couple of times. But she made it after a terrific struggle.

He came straight from the womb with a full head of shaggy

hair, looking like a Chia pet. When the nurse brought him out and showed him to me, it really knocked me silly. I'd never held a baby before, but I wanted to hold him right away. They had him wrapped up in a receiving blanket. He was no bigger than the length of my hand. He had a little red face, and little squinty eyes like shiny buttons, and all this shaggy black hair on his head. I thought he was the most beautiful thing I'd ever seen.

When we got our own apartment, things fell into place for a while. I'd given up the writing and had more time to spend with her and Keefer. I bought my first ten-speed and went for rides along the river. I joined the Y and played some pickup basketball. I felt like a new man, better and more relaxed than I'd felt in years.

I worked hard to learn the consulting business. I found out that I was good at it. About three years into it, they offered me a partnership share if I could come up with the money. They wanted $625,000. It was really a bargain. After a lot of agonizing, I went to Phil and said if he'd lend me the money, I'd pay it back in five years with interest.

"Of course I'll help you," he said.

I said, "Let's have Vinny Palumbo draw up the agreement."

Vinny was Father Palumbo's younger brother and Phil's attorney.

"What's this? A business deal? Don't get so excited. I'm happy to do this for you."

"But I want it do it right. This is a lot of money."

"Don't be excitable. We'll do it any way you like. Are you happy now?"

I said I was and he laughed and patted me on the knee and offered me a cigar.

"Always such a serious boy."

Vinny drew up the agreement that weekend and we were able to sign it before Linda, the baby, and I started back for Harrisburg. When it came time to pay back the principal five years later, I took Linda and Keefer and drove up to Bergen Cove for the weekend.

On Sunday afternoon I asked to speak to Phil in his study. When we got settled, I handed him the check. He got mad as hell. His face turned scarlet like a little baby doing a number in its pants. He scowled at the check for what seemed like a full minute, and then tore it up.

"What are you trying to tell me with this, eh? That I'm not allowed to help my own children?"

"Really, Phil. I'm grateful for all you've done over the years. I can afford to pay you back now. I've done very well, thanks to you. After all, we had an agreement--"

He stared at me until I shut up. Then his face softened and he started to cackle. He sat back and looked at me affectionately.

"Always the proud one, eh? I respect you for that. But listen: don't always push away my hand when I try to help."

"I don't, Phil. I appreciate what you've done for us."

"You're my daughter's husband. My grandson's fahdah. You're like another son to me."

"I didn't mean any disrespect."

"I know, I know. You're proud of what you made of yourself. I don't blame you. You come a long way, eh? No more lil' pot livin' in an attic somewhere. No more lil' teacher's salary, eh? A long way so fast. I tell you what to do with this money, it's so hot, it's burning a hole in your head."

"What's that?"

"Give your family a nice house to live in."

He wouldn't take the money. If I pushed, he would only get mad again.

"Okay, Phil. Whatever you say."

That's when we bought (or rather Phil's money did) the big house in Tally-Ho, a ritzy development full of doctors and lawyers north of Harrisburg, where we lived until the marriage went belly up.

We weren't happy together. But we weren't unhappy all the time, either. We just weren't well suited for each other and it made us restless and impatient. We found each other annoying. From time to time we both longed for some change in our lives, but didn't know what to do about it. We had Keefer to worry about. For a long time, he was the glue that held things together. That and Phil, who had warned me in person and by surrogate, that family was everything.

Even a bad marriage is not bad all the time. We had our good moments. Occasionally I got splattered with a little spaghetti sauce, or whatever else was handy, but not often. Sometimes we went for weeks without trouble. But in the end, what is bad is bad. You can't ever fix it, or find a real cure for it. We got on as best we could. I think I tried harder, to tell the truth. She had a careless personality. When she got mad, she didn't care what she said or did. She didn't expect me to take her seriously when she got like that. When it was over, she forgot about it. But I didn't. Some of the things she said and did bothered the hell out of me.

It wasn't the life that I'd had in mind, but it had its consolations. Keefer was the best part of it. We lived in a nice house; we had things pretty well fixed up. I liked the line of work I was in. It didn't mean a lot to me, but even that was good. It didn't hurt to do it. It didn't make me want to kill myself, the way the writing had. I could do it without a lot of grief or pain. And it paid well. That was the important thing. Reasonable compensation, I thought, for having ended up like this.

II

CHAPTER | ONE

The same summer that I tried to give Phil his money, we discovered Linda was pregnant again. Under my breath, I cursed us both for our carelessness. Keefer was eight, with all the difficulties of babyhood behind him, and we were in our thirties. I think we both secretly thought that when Keefer went off to college (in another ten years) it would be time to separate and see if we couldn't reinvent our lives. Now this accident had happened, unthinkable, given the frugal amount of passion we spent in each other's arms, and it would tack at least another eighteen years onto our tepid marriage. Besides, on some unconscious level I think we both realized that as long as Phil was around, neither one of us would have the courage to make a move. He was such a force in our lives; it was impossible for either of us weaklings to think of making any major changes without his permission. Linda was pregnant. We had a beautiful house and a beautiful boy. We were stuck, until death do us part. Phil's death, I mean.

After we were certain, and before we told anyone, we discussed the possibility of an abortion. It was never really an option. As I have said, Linda was not especially religious. But she was sufficiently superstitious to think that if she went against the church's teaching in so grave a matter, something horrible might happen to us.

"Besides, how would Daddy feel if he ever found out?"

Right, I thought. Until his death do us part.

When Linda told Phil the news, he went out of his mind with happiness. He bought a farm out on the North Fork and a couple of ponies so the kids could be raised in the fresh air. When he announced this on one of our visits to Bergen Cove, I looked at Linda, and she grinned and shrugged her shoulders, as though to say, *Gee, what can you do when somebody takes over your life?*

Keefer was almost as happy as Phil. When we told him, he hopped around the house singing, "I hope it's a bruth-thah, I hope it's a bruth-thah."

When I called Nola and told her, there was a pause on the line. Then in a faint voice I heard her croak, "Oh no."

"'Oh no'? What is that supposed to mean?"

"I only meant that one child is probably enough in this day and age, what with all the wars and bombs and everything. I think we'll blow ourselves up before the end of the century, don't you?"

"Ma. You're supposed to be happy."

"I am, dear. I hope it's a girl this time. You were supposed to be a girl. Look how that turned out."

"Okay, Ma. I'll see you soon."

And thanks for filling me with dread.

Linda was thirty-five. Not exactly the ideal age for childbearing. Especially considering the tough time she'd had with Keefer. But this time the pregnancy sped along, smooth and uneventful. The baby was due just before Christmas, according to Linda's obstetrician, Dr. Monaghan. He was an elderly gentleman whom Linda admired for his courtly manners. He was flirtatious too, in a geriatrically formal sort of way. His ancient nurse was rarely in the room when he examined Linda. It didn't bother her, though. She said if he tried anything funny, she'd give him a good punch in the nose like she did me back in our college days when I tried to get "fresh," as she put it.

The old fool listened to her tummy through something that resembled a bugle. He made her put on a little examining gown that didn't close properly at the back and looked her up and down when she stepped on the weighing scales. From the back, she didn't look pregnant. This angle allowed his imagination freer play, she supposed.

"If it gives him a thrill to peek at my backside, let him. He's old and lonely. He hasn't got a wife or anything. Not even any kids. I feel sorry for him."

She liked the old geezer. She was touched by his gentle, faintly prurient grandfatherly manner. She didn't mind it when he patted her knee or accidentally put his hand on her can as he escorted her down the hall. Often, as they sat in the quiet fugitive shadows of his inner sanctum at the back of the building, where the dusty blinds limited the light to a few golden strokes on the thread-bare carpet, the muted sounds of traffic from the distant street reminded her of the surf in the little cove behind Phil's house. It made her feel so relaxed, so secure, so much at home. The tottery old doctor, such a sweet old thingy really, would look up from her file, smile dimly between the stacks of unread medical journals collecting dust on his desk, and gently wag his finger.

"Now now, my pet. We're gaining a tad too much weight, I fear."

She developed a little double chin. With her round face and pug nose and short-cut curly black hair, she looked like a baby herself. Her belly swelled into the shape of a gibbous moon: tight as a drum, heavy and uncomfortable with the burgeoning lump of baby coiled inside. I watched her belly button slowly disappear. It left behind a brown spot the size of a silver dollar, like a bruise in a piece of fruit. When instructed, I bent and listened to the gurgly waters. Once I was kicked in the ear for my trouble.

I bought her maternity tops and dresses to replace the ones she'd given away after Keefer was born. I helped her on with those horrible slacks with the special elastic panel in the front as she sat on the bed and groaned about her back and swollen legs. I listened to her complain about her sore nipples. I gave up sex. No sacrifice, I admit, since I lacked enthusiasm to make love to a woman who looked more each day like Babe Ruth at the end of his playing days. When nudged, I got up in the middle of the night. I fetched her ice water and the peppermint patties she kept hidden from Keefer in the liquor cabinet in the study. I did everything I could, short of showing any real enthusiasm.

She said every man should have such nice manners and gentle ways with women as Dr. Monaghan, but I noticed the old gentleman's kindly admonitions didn't affect her eating habits. She put on a lot of weight with this pregnancy. Especially during the last three weeks of her term, after Phil and Mario and Cousin Vito came down to lend moral support and be on hand for the baby's arrival, and "the boys," as she called them, took over the cooking chores.

Phil and his posse took rooms at the Penn Motel, about a mile from the house, much to Linda's chagrin. She wanted them to cancel their reservations and stay at our place.

"Come on, Daddy. We want you here with us, don't we, Earl? Don't insult us like this."

Over the years she'd picked up some of his rhetorical tricks. I made polite noises in my throat. She kept insisting at the dinner table on the first night of their visit that they stay with us. Phil made a face as if he'd bitten into something rotten and waved her off with a stalk of celery.

"Enough! Don't aggravate me wid talk about this!"

When he saw her eyes fill with tears, he laid the celery stalk on the tablecloth, patted her hand, and spoke more gently.

"Listen to me, eh? Be a good lil' girl and listen to what I say. I know you 'n' Ur like us here wid you. Sure, sure, you do, I know. But I got a bad cough now, eh? I don't sleep so well at nights. Ever since your poor mother died, I don't sleep for nuthin'. I gotta sit up in a chair with this cough. Ask your brother 'n' Cousin Vito. Eh? Do I sleep anymore?"

Phil studied them severely. Mario and Cousin Vito obediently swiveled their heads no. He gave them a dismissive grunt and turned his attention back to Linda.

"Besides, we gonna go to the track some nights. I don't wanna come and go disturbing everybody. How would it be to wake the baby every night, eh? Not so good."

Even though Keefer was eight, he still referred to him as "the baby."

"You want to go to the track in December? You'll catch pneumonia."

"Yaah," he waved her off with his celery again. "We stay in a warm pot."

By which he meant they would sit in the enclosed grandstand and not lean against the rail on the homestretch, where he liked to install himself in the good weather. Even though it hurt her feelings, his decision to stay at the motel made little difference. Except for one or two nights, they were always at our house until one or two o'clock in the morning. I found myself wishing the baby would hurry up, so Phil and his entourage would go home. I was tired of the company: the late hours; the cigar smoke; all the booze and the sumptuous meals that Mario and Cousin Vito insisted on preparing for us night after night; the endless gravelly table talk about horses and the New York Mets.

Certainly the visit was good for Linda. She seemed happier than she'd been for months. It was not an unmixed blessing. With all the wine at every meal and a steady regimen of after dinner drinks, she was often crocked by seven o'clock. We were an ignorant lot back in those days. Few people were aware of the possible ill effects on the fetus that alcohol and smoking could cause. I don't think Monaghan ever said a word to her about it.

She made for a sloppy drunk, slurred her words, spilled food down the front of her clothes, burned holes in the tablecloth with her cigarettes, and sat there with an elbow on the table, wearing a rubbery smile on her face. I knew better than to tell her to ease up, what with so much spaghetti sauce and so many pasta dishes ready at hand. She was more likely to let fly when she'd had a couple of drinks. I didn't fancy getting splattered in front of Phil and the boys.

Cousin Vito drove her to her appointments with Dr. Monaghan. She said the old guy was trying to get her to call him Dr. Tom. He said it was what he liked all his favorite patients to call him. She told him she wouldn't feel right about it. She didn't think it showed the proper respect. He gingerly looped an arm around her. His hand strayed for a moment onto her swollen breast: the age-old ploy of a horny adolescent. Of course he removed it at once.

"But I insist, my dear," he said with a courtly bow.

"Okay, I'll try."

But she could never bring herself to do it. She went on calling him Dr. Monaghan, but now with a smirk she could barely repress, and the old fool went on insisting that she should call him Dr. Tom.

"That's what all my friends call me," he kept repeating in a wistful voice.

"Can you imagine?" she told me with a shy smile that made her lips tremble. "I think he'd like to fool around after I have the baby. I wonder if he gets this silly with all his expectant mothers?"

"If he's annoying you--"

"Oh no! If you said anything to him, I know it would absolutely crush him. He's perfectly harmless. I feel sorry for him. He must be awful lonely. I think he's kind of sweet, actually."

I shrugged and thought no more about it. I saw no harm in the man, if she didn't. Poor Linda. She must have been so hungry for affection. I was spending next to no time at home. Always out on meetings, or on the road. Arthur and I and the rest of the staff were working hard. The business was thriving. It was taking us up and down the Eastern Seaboard, and as far away as Chicago and Kansas City. Work was a wonderful excuse to concentrate elsewhere. It was no wonder she didn't mind if Monaghan's hand occasionally strayed to her backside. It was more attention than she got from me.

This didn't escape Phil's notice. One night after dinner, he said he wanted to talk to me privately. We went into the study under the pretext of having a shot or two of Grappa together. Linda had wearily plodded upstairs to help Keefer get ready for bed. Mario and Cousin Vito were off cleaning up the mess they had made of the kitchen. We settled into our chairs.

"Well, well," said Phil, admiring his surroundings. "You come a long way. Look at this, eh?"

"Yeah, now I have all these books, and no time to read them."

"Aah, books!" he made a face. "But this house, eh? A big job. A beautiful baby boy. A good wife–"

I nodded my head, agreeing with everything he said. Yes indeed, I had it made. He extracted a crooked black cigar from his inside coat pocket and lit it with one of the wooden matches he carried loose among the change in his pants pocket. He scratched the match alive on his horny thumbnail. He cupped it between his petrified fingers and stiffly bent his face closer to the flame. The light from the lamp on the table behind him put his face in shadow. The match flared and dimmed in tiny duplicate pinpoints in the black shiny minus signs of his pupils, throwing into relief his flattened nose and deep-set eyes squinting against the match and the deeply scored lines that set in parentheses his wide mouth. He got the cigar going and sat back in his chair with a satisfied growl. He puffed on it rapidly, as if keeping tempo with the thoughts percolating in his brain.

He seemed nervous. He was a twitchy fellow anyway. Sometimes this twitchiness bothered him so much that for relief he felt obliged to ventilate a little spleen on Mario or Cousin Vito, or one of the other men who were always hanging around his house. One day at Bergen Cove, I saw him practically run across the kitchen floor and kick Mario square in the seat of his pants. He was setting down some bags of groceries on the kitchen table. Phil's foot to his seat straightened him up and nearly lifted him off the floor. It must have hurt like hell. Mario wanted to know what he'd done wrong.

"Nuthin'," Phil said, looking a little ashamed of himself. "I'm ah jumpy. I hadda do somethin'." Then the old fierceness returned and he scowled, "I seen beddah lookin' donkeys than you! Get away from me before I put a shoe up-ah you ass!"

Sometimes he turned his irritability against himself. This took the form of dissatisfaction with some item of his clothing. Either his shirt was too tight under the arms, or across his pigeon-breasted chest, or the shirttail wouldn't stay jammed into the back of his pants as it was supposed to. Now and then when he stood up fast, his underwear cut him in the crotch, making him cry out in a strangled voice as if an assassin had just stabbed him.

Tonight, it looked like his argyle sweater was the culprit. He kept plucking it at with his free hand. First under the arms and then at his breastbone, in a more less regular pattern of irritability, as if signing the cross in a particularly idiosyncratic manner. Finally he settled down. He took the cigar out of his mouth. He swirled his Grappa and took a good swallow. He smacked his lips and showed me all the yellowed ivory of his peg teeth in that scrimshaw grin of his. As always, the muscles in his cheeks forced his narrow yellow eyes shut, as if he couldn't bear to look at me and smile at the same time.

"Linda says lots of nights you're out on business. A lot of travel out of town. Meetin's 'n' stuff."

"Yes," I shook my head as if it were regrettable. "We're really busy at the office. Business is up thirty percent over last year."

"Good, good. I'm so happy everything is coming up flowers. Linda tells me you think about writing another book."

A thin complicitous grin spread over his face from ear to ear.

"Whatsamaddah? You don't have enough to keep you busy?"

I gave it my best self-deprecating little chuckle.

"I haven't started anything. I probably won't."

"How many hours you work now?"

"I probably bill fifty or sixty hours a week. Of course, I can't bill for everything."

Phil favored me with one of his irrepressible cackles.

"You wanna be rich or somethin'?"

I smiled, "I wouldn't mind."

"Listen to me. Don't be offended if I give you some advice. May I share with you what's in my heart?"

"Of course."

"Thank you. I know how proud you are. That's why I ask. I

know how hard you work. You could be my own blood son, and I couldn't love you more, or be prouder of you than I am. You understand what I'm saying?"

"Phil, you're like a father to me. I–"

"Excuse me, if you don't mind shuttin' up, please. I gotta finish what I'm sayin' before I forget. Please don't take-ah the fence by this."

"No offense taken."

"Good, good. Listen to me. It's nice you work so hard. But Keeper, he's growing up widout a fahdah. Linda's lonely too, eh? Look at her face, you can tell. She says nothing. I can see for myself."

"I know I'm not spending much time with them–"

"Now a new baby is coming. What you gonna do? Let your children grow up like monkeys in a jungle?"

He rumbled a little in his chest and coughed out a watery gasp or two, so I'd know he was trying to be funny.

"Listen to me. Work is good. Too much is bad. Always your family should come first. The country is going to hell because the people forget this simple truth. I wish I could go back 'n' spend time with my kids when they was lil'. I shoulda spent more time with my wife, may the Mother of God forgive me. Now she's dead. I can go to the track whenever I want. I got plenty a time. I can go to the cemetery and talk to her tombstone, if I want. You see how sorry you can be? I'm an old man. Excuse me, but I know what I'm talking about. I wanna be sure you understand."

"I do, Phil. I appreciate your concern."

He pointed his cigar at me sternly.

"The family, you understand?"

"Right, Phil."

His face softened.

"Don't worry," he smiled. "When God calls me, I make you rich."

I didn't know what to say. "Thank you" seemed inadequate. It didn't even seem appropriate. I nodded my head, returned his benevolent look, and waited politely for what he'd say next. He let the promise of my future riches sink in for a minute.

"When the baby's old enough, take Linda away somewhere nice, eh? You know how she likes fancy places. It would be a nice thing to do. You can leave Keeper 'n' the new baby wid us. Who knows more about babies 'n' Anna? It'll be like a second honeymoon. Only this time, with plenty of money and no worries. Maybe you wanna go back to Bermuda. What a nice time, eh? That's where you made your son, such a fine strong boy. Maybe all that sunshine did it for you. Maybe you wanna go back. Who knows? Maybe this time you make a couple of twins, eh? I'd be greatly honored to pay for such a trip. It would be such a pleasure for me. A lil' anniversary present to give you kids early for a change."

I thanked him for his advice. I tried to be polite without outright refusing his offer. I was tempted to say: Listen, Phil. Listen to *me,* for a change. A second honeymoon won't fix what's wrong with us. If we spend more time together, it'll only get worse, not better. Can't you see? We're living together in the only way we can. But I didn't say any of that. Instead, I nodded my head solemnly. I agreed that a little more time together ought to do it, that plus spending a couple of grand at some luxurious watering hole, where the food was fattening, the golfing good, and the sun shone all the time. Give him credit. He was not easily discouraged.

Although he was never outright threatening, I felt these coaching sessions about my responsibilities to the family were growing more menacing. I wondered where it was going to end. What would happen to me if he finally lost patience? I didn't want to get in any deeper; I didn't want to owe him anything more. I was already in over my head. But I had one thing going for me: I knew nothing about Phil's businesses, what was legit, what was off the books, what politicians were on the take, who was on the payroll, none of that, and I meant to keep it that way. Yet if he was finished with me, I knew my ignorance would offer scant protection.

Phil and the boys had been hovering on the scene like a bad parody of the three wise men for nearly three weeks when one night, at three o'clock in the morning, with snow mixed with sleet whispering like sand against the windows, Linda woke me with a powerful nudge in the ribs.

"Huh? Is it time?"

"Naw. I thought you'd like to play a hand of gin rummy."

"Ha. Very funny."

She snapped on the light and we rolled out of bed. I was out in the hall, groping my way to the bathroom, when I heard her say, "Hi, Daddy. I'm ready."

He had insisted that we call, no matter what the hour.

I came back into the room, pulled a shirt and pair of pants over my pajamas, and got her suitcase out of the closet.

"Turn on the porch light for Daddy."

"Boy, what a lousy night."

"I didn't *plan* it this way."

"Okay, don't get excited."

"Well don't give me any junk."

Downstairs, it was cold and damp in the hallway and the wind was booming against the front door. I got my overcoat and Bean boots out of the closet, put them on, and sat down on the stairs to wait for her. I hoped it wouldn't take Phil and the boys too long to get here. With the wind blowing like that, the roads were sure to start drifting shut in places. She was in the bathroom for what seemed like hours. When she came downstairs, she was still in her robe and slippers.

"Aren't you going to get dressed?"

"Why bother? I'll only have to peel again. Isn't Daddy here yet?"

"Not yet."

"Good, I'm hungry."

"What do you mean, you're hungry?"

"Move. I want some ice cream."

"Linda, you're having a baby. You can't go into this on a full stomach."

"Don't worry. Ice cream melts fast."

She was standing in the doorway to the kitchen, spooning in the last of the French vanilla straight from the carton, when Phil arrived. He cackled behind a spotted hand that looked like a garden claw.

"You love to eat, don't you, baby girl? Heh-heh. Come on, dahlin'."

"You'll get a fat ass, Sis."

"You should talk, Tubbo."

Cousin Vito dug me in the ribs.

"Happy Fahdah's Day, Pops."

He had the babysitting assignment. Grinning sleepily, he crossed the living room carpet, ground out his cigarette in the ashtray on the coffee table, stripped off his overcoat, and covered himself with it as he stretched full length on the couch. He shut his eyes. His horse face took on an expression slumberous and tranquil, like a stone effigy atop a medieval sarcophagus.

"Come on! Come on! Let's go!"

At the sound of Phil's voice, Mario seized the overnight bag and led the way out the door. He hunched his balding head against the sleet as he stepped from the porch onto the walk, coated with snow that looked as slippery as soap powder. In the shafts of light from the windows and the doorway, the sleet came shawling down out of the darkness like showers of diamond dust.

Phil's big car was idling in the driveway. He and I followed Mario down the walk, helping Linda. She had her mink coat thrown over her shoulders like a movie star on the way to a premiere. Phil ordered me into the car first, so she could sit between us. By the time we got her in and settled, the hem of her robe and gown were soaking wet and plastered to her ankles. Her slippers were ruined too.

"It looks like those slippers have had it."

"Don't make a fuss about it. They're only cheap things."

"Take them off and tuck your feet in the car robe. You don't want to catch pneumonia."

I was disgusted with her. She could have taken a second to put on a pair of boots, instead of going out into the snow like that. That airy carelessness of hers toward such mundane matters as slippers, so long as someone else was footing the bills, never sat well with me.

Phil snapped on the TV. I opened the bar, splashed some brandy in a glass for him, and poured some vodka over ice for myself.

"What about me? Aren't you going to offer me anything?"

"Linda: you're going to have a baby."

"Well, it's still rude of you not to offer me anything."

Phil laughed around the edges of the cigar between his teeth.

"Umm-umm-urrh-urrh," he rumbled. A noise supposedly mirthful, but played at the wrong speed. We settled back. We watched John Wayne being heroic on the TV. Mario cautiously manipulated the big heavy car through the swirling mixture of snow and sleet and the drifts forming in the streets. The wind was still blowing hard. No other cars were on the road. Linda had her head on my shoulder and her hand between the buttons of my overcoat. When an especially bad contraction convulsed her, she let me know by digging her fingers into my side.

"Ow! That hurts."

"You should be on this end, bud."

Phil started to get nervous. He rattled the ice cubes in his glass. He puffed on his cigar. His eyes shifted from side to side. His forehead began to shine with perspiration.

"What's taking so long?"

"Pop, I've got to go slow on a night like this. Look at it out there."

"Hurry up! Before your sistah drops it on the floor back here!"

Linda patted his hand, "Don't worry, Daddy. We got plenty of time."

Finally the car crept up to the front door of the hospital. A little welcoming party was waiting for us. Through the glass doors, I saw Monaghan holding his white head erect, standing next to a nurse with a wheelchair, who moved forward smartly the moment the car stopped. She and I got Linda into the chair and in through the doors. The nurse was about to take off with her across the lobby when Linda made her stop and turn the chair around.

"You guys wait for me. No matter how long it takes. You wait right here. Don't go running off somewhere. Don't do the big male thing, and go off for a drink or out to breakfast or something. Okay?"

She said it with such childlike seriousness it made us laugh, including Monaghan.

"Haw-haw. Don't worry, my dear. You're in my hands now. You can be sure I'll take good care of you."

"Don't go away. Promise," she said to me.

I kissed her forehead and assured her we weren't going anywhere. Then the nurse whisked her away. When I introduced Monaghan to Phil he said, "You have a beautiful daughter, sir," and squeezed Phil's arthritic hand for emphasis.

He dawdled with us for a few minutes while we waited for Mario to come in from the parking lot.

"Well, sir. Duty calls. We don't want to keep your grandchild waiting, do we? Haw-haw!"

He set off slowly across the open stretches of terrazzo floor between the islands of orange and yellow Naugahyde chairs and sofas that stretched in a long archipelago across the lobby toward the polished black granite banks of elevators. Eventually he wandered out of sight.

"Damn fool, isn't he? Linda thinks he's wonderful."

We were the only ones in the waiting room. Somewhere down the hall, a radio full of static faded in and out, quavering out Christmas carols from two stations at once. It annoyed me to the point of lunacy. I was tempted to go down the hall and tell them to fix it or turn it the fuck off.

Phil was jumpy too. After a few minutes he began to growl at Mario.

"Why you breathin' so hard all the time? You got somethin'

wrong with your nose?"

"I'm sitting here, Pop. Minding my own business."

"Look at you," Phil said in disgust. "You're gettin' fat like a pig."

"Come on, Pop. Pick on Earl for a change."

It seemed we barely settled in before I looked up and was surprised to see Monaghan hesitating in the doorway. He looked silly in his green cap and surgical gown, like an amateur thespian got up to play the part of the doctor in a French farce. But his face was gray and troubled, and it brought me straight up out of my seat. He tottered two steps into the room, reached out uncertainly, and dropped a vague hand on my sleeve. Behind his glasses his pale-blue watery eyes were shiny as wet shellac.

"I'm afraid I have bad news. Your wife--"

"Oh my God! Something's happened to Linda?"

"Oh no no. She's fine. But I'm afraid we've-- I'm afraid we've lost the baby."

I turned and walked directly across the room into the telephone booth and pulled the door shut behind me. Mario followed after me and threw himself against the door and yipped like a puppy. I bent over and hid my face and rocked back and forth and cried. I heard a commotion outside. I looked up. Phil and Monaghan seemed to be dancing geriatrically around the room. But they weren't dancing; far from it. Monaghan's mouth hung open in terror as he struggled to free Phil's grip on his windpipe. I opened the door and pushed Mario aside to get them apart.

"Goddam you quack bastard! I kill you for this!"

Phil swung wildly and caught me a glancing blow on the ear. The three of us staggered like a badly coordinated chorus line.

"Let go, Phil. He can't breathe."

"My grandson can't breathe needah!"

He shook Monaghan as a terrier might a rat. Finally Monaghan and I loosened Phil's death grip on his throat, and with his gown in shreds he fled the room.

I went down the hall to get away from Phil's voice. Mario was trying to settle him down and Phil was cursing him and slapping him around the room. He sounded like a man who'd been cheated and was going to make a scene until the management refunded the last six hours of his life. I moved out of range of their voices into the foyer and rested my head against the wall by the elevators.

"Mr. Bogwell?"

A flustered nurse stood a few feet behind me, wringing her hands.

"Dr. Monaghan would like to see you, sir."

She led me down another hall and through some swinging doors with porthole windows into a cold barren general office area. He was sitting at a small metal desk, nursing a cup of coffee, trying to recover his dignity. He stood up when he saw me.

"This is terrible."

He offered me a khaki-colored stool with a perforated metal seat to sit on. He told me again how sorry he was. Then he looked at the floor.

"Nothing like this has ever happened to me in forty-four years of medical practice. I've never been--manhandled by a member of a patient's family before."

"I apologize for him. Family is everything to him. He's very upset."

Monaghan shook his head sadly

"The child was perfectly formed."

He shook his head again.

"I don't understand it. Apparently it was dead for some hours, by the condition of the skin. I thought I had a heart beat. I'm very sorry."

"I know you are."

"Will you explain to him that it was stillborn? There wasn't anything I could do?"

"Yes, I'll tell him."

"He's very angry."

"Yes he is. I'll explain it wasn't your fault."

"Thank you. I would talk to him myself, I'm afraid–"

"You're right. He's too upset."

"It wouldn't do any good?"

"No, I'm afraid it wouldn't."

"I don't understand it. Your wife has a beautiful body for child-bearing. Nice breasts and wide hips–"

He gazed across the room at some private vision growing cold on the wall. He jerked upright in his chair as if recollecting I was still there.

"May I offer you a cup of coffee?"

"No thanks. Maybe I'd better see my wife."

"Of course. How stupid of me to keep you like this. I'll have the nurse take you in. Will you authorize an autopsy? I recommend it. We should try to find the reasons for this."

Blindly, I scratched my name on the necessary papers.

"How would you like to handle the body?"

I was unsure of his meaning, and must have looked it.

"Sometimes the family wants a funeral," he explained. "Other times, they want us to take care of it for them."

"Yes, you take care of it."

"That's what I would recommend."

"How--?"

"Cremation. I'll have the nurse take you in now. I'm so sorry."

He stood up and shook my hand. He flashed me a tremulous smile full of yellow horse teeth. He looked as though he was ready to cry. I nodded, returned the pressure of his handshake, and patted him on the shoulder. As he turned away, he showed me the saddest smile I have ever seen in my life.

I trailed down the hall after the nurse. I felt as if I'd been beaten with a broomstick. She was no taller than a high hurdle. Her feet moved in parallel steps like a chimpanzee's. I watched her muscular calves, clad in hose as deathly white as a mime's greasepaint. The only sound in the passageway was the squeak of her crepe soles on the polished floor.

Linda lay under a rumpled sheet on a gurney in one of the recovery rooms. Her green gown was soaked with sweat; her thick black curly hair was still pasted to her forehead.

As I hugged her she whispered, "Did you see him?"

"No."

"He was beautiful. He had a lovely straight nose like yours--"

She cupped her palms over her face and began to cry. When I tried to hold her again, she shook her head and held me off with her hands on my chest.

"Please don't hug me. I feel like I'm going to suffocate. Let me get over this in my own way."

"Whatever you say."

"How's Daddy taking it?"

"Bad. He tried to throttle Monaghan. Mario's trying to calm him down."

"Poor Daddy. You better take him home."

"I think I should stay with you. Mario can take him home."

"No, you go with them. He'll just give Mario hell for everything. He'll calm down if you're there."

"Are you sure?"

She gave me a brave smile.

"Come back this afternoon, okay? I promise I'll act better when I've had some sleep."

It was midmorning before we got home. Keefer greeted us at the door.

"Where's Mommy and the baby?"

Phil emitted a grunt of sympathy and reached for his cigars.

"She'll be home in a few days. The doctors didn't have any babies for us this time."

"Darn," he said.

I got down on my knees. Automatically he walked into my arms and laid his head against my chest. I loved him so much in that moment for his faith in the feeble answers we supplied to his unanswerable questions.

Later that night when I put him to bed we had another talk. I was about to step out of his room and I was looking forward to going downstairs and having a couple of stiff drinks with Phil and the boys.

"Daddy?"

"What is it, son?"

"Who killed the baby?"

I crossed the room and sat down on his bed. By the faint glow of the nightlight, I saw that grave baby face that he had inherited from his mother, looking up at me solemnly from his pillows. I smoothed his hair back from his forehead.

"Nobody killed the baby, honey. It was born dead. I told you that."

"Yeah but–how could it be born, if it was dead? Don't you have to be alive to be born?"

"Well--not always."

He took my hand and studied my knuckles with a puzzled expression.

"Was it a boy?"

"Yes, it was."

"Darn. I wanted a brother."

"Maybe you'll have one someday."

"What are you and Mommy going to do now?"

"What do you mean, what are we going to do?"

"Are you going to get a divorce or something?"

"No, of course not, baby. Everything's fine. There's nothing for you to worry about."

"Your voice sounds sad."

"I am sad. But I'll get over it. So will your mother. You'll have to help us, okay?"

"Okay."

"Now go to sleep. And don't worry so much. Leave that for the grown-ups."

"I love you, Daddy."

"I love you too, baby."

CHAPTER | TWO

The day we picked up Linda at the hospital, she was wearing the black wool suit that I always thought looked so good on her. Her glossy black hair was pulled back into a chignon at the base of her neck. She looked morose and severely beautiful, and as she slid off the bed onto her feet, I tried to put my arms around her, but she held me off. Her face was white and trembling.

"How could you let them cremate him?"

It really caught me by surprise.

"How could you let them burn him like a piece of garbage? Get away from me."

Phil heard the last of this as he limped up on his bandy-legged rocking-horse walk. His sunken cheeks and stringy neck instantly mottled the color of burgundy wine.

"Whatsamaddah for you? Be nice to your husband! You think only you got a right to feel bad?"

"Daddy."

She held out her arms to him helplessly. Seeing it was a serious matter, he passed the stub of his wet cigar to Mario and gave her a hug that was all elbows. The back of his baldhead gleamed like the knob on top of a walnut newel post.

"Whatsamaddah, lil' girl?"

He patted her between the shoulder blades.

"Oh Daddy."

Her head dropped to his shoulder, as if she hadn't the strength to hold it up any longer. She began to cry--hard, racking sobs that shook her whole body. Phil patted her and waited. Mario slung his arm around me and gave me a consolatory thump or two on the shoulder.

When she raised her head again, her cheeks were muddy with mascara. She wiped away the dirty tears with the backs of her hands. She plucked at his lapels.

"Why did this have to happen?"

He laughed, a sound harsh and guttural.

"God don't tell me his secrets, dahlin'."

She hid her face again in the front of his coat, but she was calmer now. She was sniffling, trying to catch her breath. With his stiff gray fingers, he raised her chin.

"Come on, come on. You're making a big mess of your face, eh? You cry so hard, all the pencil marks run down your cheeks."

"Oh Daddy, I want to go home. I want to sleep in my own bed. Where's Keefer? Where's my baby boy?"

"Cousin Vito's watchin' him. We thought maybe the hospital would scare 'im."

"Dear sweet Daddy."

We went down the corridor together and got in the elevator. While Mario and I attended to the billing and followed with the bags, she walked out of the hospital on her father's arm.

"Don't worry," said Mario. "She'll get over it."

I wasn't particularly worried. At that point, I wanted to give her a good swift kick in the ass. *You think only you got a right to feel bad?* When we got home, she sank to her knees on the living room rug and greeted Keefer with a silent ferocious hug. Over her shoulder he gave me a bewildered look. I tried to reassure him with a little encouraging nod.

"What's wrong, Mommy?"

Her eyes filled with tears as she held him away and smiled at him.

"Nothing, baby. Mommy's so glad to see you, that's all."

She gave him another fierce hug. He looked utterly confused by this form of happiness. I thought she ought to try to buck up for his sake. But she was always very open with him when it came to her feelings. She considered it a point of moral superiority never to hold anything back from him. She called it being honest; but it wasn't being honest. It was careless and irresponsible and self indulgent. Nothing else.

Shortly afterward, claiming exhaustion, she went upstairs to rest in our room with the shades drawn against the afternoon light.

That night, it was Cousin Vito's turn to make dinner. When it was ready, Phil shuffled into the hallway and shouted up the stairs.

"Linda dahlin'!"

No answer.

"Linda!"

"What, Daddy?" came the faint reply.

"You comin' down for dinner?"

"I don't think so, Daddy."

"Come on, baby. Cousin Vito make-ah duck special for you."

"I'm not hungry, Daddy."

"We gotta ice cream for dessert."

"Maybe I'll come down for ice cream and coffee later."

"Okay, honeybun."

As he turned from the stairs the targets of his yellow eyes met mine. He bobbed his head and smiled his crocodile smile.

"It's okay. Coupla days, she be all right. She's young. Strong. Soon you make another baby together. She forget about this. 'S true."

He expected me to agree immediately. He waited for some sign that, like him, I understood the way things were. When it wasn't forthcoming, he sighed and jerked his head, signifying that the least I could do was lead the way into the dining room.

Everything was simple to him--stark, but simple. He believed suffering was the natural lot of women, that it was a foolish waste of time, and men should have none of it. It was what women did best, and what men shouldn't do at all. When things went wrong, women wept and wrung their hands, and appealed to Providence for relief. It was altogether fitting for them to do so, part of the natural confederacy that existed between home and Father Palumbo's church, with all the nice statuary tucked away in the back garden. Women cried for the men, so the men didn't have to cry for themselves. The men were therefore freed to deal with each other: to seek redress for indignities; to assign blame; to engage in the appropriate acts of retribution. Even if sometimes it only amounted to grabbing an old fool by his lapels and spraying him with curses full of spittle and nicotine.

The dining room was humid and odoriferous with rosemary and garlic and other spices intermingling over the steaming platters of food that Cousin Vito, wearing a full white apron, was setting on the table. He bent stiffly from the waist as he reverently put them down, as if bowing in turn to each of his specialties. The old man had outdone himself. He had food enough to feed even a fair-sized contingent of the far flung Gagliano family, should members of the clan suddenly decend out of the ether.

"There!"

He stood back to admire the loaded table and proudly wiped his hands on his apron.

"Whaddya think of this, eh?"

A triumph of platters and tureens steamed on the cloth like a miniature industrial complex: linguine with duck *confit* prepared in his secret game sauce; macaroni and sausage in tomato sauce; a big salad of lettuce and tomato and onions and green and red peppers, garnished with anchovies; a steaming bowl of broccoli and fresh mushrooms; tomatoes with fresh garlic and hearts of palm in olive oil and vinegar; *pappardelle Bolognese*; a tureen of seafood chowder containing chunks of lobster, clams, mussels, and three kinds of fish. Everybody murmured growls of appreciation as Cousin Vito stood there beaming at us, with tomato sauce staining the bib of his apron.

"It's beautiful," I told him. " You've outdone yourself, Cousin Vito."

As Phil approached the table, he had another one of his hot flashes. But his fingers were too stiff to work the snap buttons on his plaid shirt and he was unable to get out of it by himself. After thrashing about for a few minutes, he growled, "Goddam this ting! Somebody get it off!"

He hunched on his chair in exasperated impatience, snarling and cursing, as Mario tried to unsnap and strip the shirt off his stump-like torso and nearly useless arms.

"Vito! Let Cousin Vito do it. You don't know how to do nuthin'."

"You don't need Cousin Vito. Hold still for a second."

"*Stupido!* Holy Mother of God, you give me a son like this!"

After the crisis was over, and with a smidgen of his dignity restored, he sat at the head of the table in his ribbed undershirt, his arms propped on the tablecloth. I noticed he was developing little conical mounds of flesh, like undifferentiated nipples, on the ends of his elbows. They stuck out in little tits even when he straightened out his arms. No end to the indignities, I thought. They keep coming, faster and thicker, the older you grow.

I remembered something Nola had said to me a few weeks past, when I'd visited her. She had drawn my attention to her hands. The skin was loose and waxen. She'd lost a good deal of weight in the past year. "Look at this," she pinched the skin on the back of her hand. It stayed pinched up in a little soft ridge until she smoothed it out again.

"Isn't that wonderful? I sag in all directions. I've got purple scribbly marks all over my legs, like somebody used me for grafitti. I'll tell you, life is really something. If you're unlucky, they put you in a box and stick you in the ground while you're still young and presentable. But if you're lucky, you get to be old and ugly like me."

She gave me a big sour grin.

"Isn't life great?"

It was better to be hard as agate, like Phil, instead of soft like Nola. I hadn't called her yet about the baby, and I was dreading it. We passed the dishes back and forth. I watched Phil out of the sides of my eyes. Moodily, he relit his cigar, which had gone out in the ashtray during the struggle with his shirt.

"How about some duck, Pop?"

"I can't eat nuthin'. Maybe a lil' salad. A lil' glass of wine. Nuthin' tastes good to me no more."

We received this ritual remark in the usual silence and, as if that were the signal, we began to eat. I had no particular appetite either, but I knew I couldn't refuse Cousin Vito's meal without giving insult. It would be like returning a funeral wreath and saying to the sender, "Thanks, but I don't care for flowers."

Phil, of course, was allowed to abstain from the feast. He could do anything he wanted. His authority superseded all the requirements of custom, even in matters dealing with death. So I ate, as courtesy required. I ate the vast amount of food that Cousin Vito tenderly heaped for me on my plate. I told him everything was delicious, and he was pleased. I asked for seconds, requesting "just a little this time," since courtesy now permitted it. And we ate together, passing the wine back and forth, and limiting our remarks mainly to compliments about the food and drink.

We found relief in fussing over Keefer. We tucked his napkin into his shirt so he wouldn't get anything on his new cowboy suit. We spooned the lobster out of the stew for him. We gave him the choicest bits of the duck. When he complained that it was too spicy, we wiped the sauce off the meat for him.

"How's that, my little prince?"

"Much better, peasant. What's for dessert?"

He rewarded us by singing a song that he'd learned in school. In a high trebly voice, with his napkin still tucked in his shirt, he sang to us:

"Oh, Senor Don Gato was a cat,
On a high red roof Don Gato sat.
He went there to read a letter,
Meow, meow, meow
Where the reading light was better,
Meow, meow, meow

'Twas a love note for Don Gato!

Naturally he had to sing all the verses to us, including the part where Don Gato in his happiness falls off the roof and breaks all his whiskers and his little solar plexus, and how the doctors are sent for, but can't save the poor fellow, and how on the way to the cemetery as the funeral procession passes through the market square, the little caballero cat is miraculously revived by the smell of fresh fish in the air.

It was funny and charmed us silly. We all laughed harder than we should have, for reasons other than the song. Then, flushed with success, he took his napkin out of the front of his cowboy shirt and made a droopy big bow of it and held it to the side of his head, and said in a helpless soprano:

"I can't pay the rent!"

He held the napkin under his nose, where it became a droopy mustache. He frowned and said in the deepest voice he could muster:

"But you must pay the rent!"

The napkin became a hair ribbon again.

"But I can't pay the rent!"

"But you must pay the rent!"

"But I can't pay the rent!"

The napkin became a bow tie.

"I'll pay the rent!"

A hair ribbon again.

"My hero!"

We all laughed at this performance too. What a relief it was to laugh. Having exhausted his repertoire of songs and theatrical set pieces, he slipped off with me to the living room while Mario and Cousin Vito cleared the table and fetched the coffee and dessert, and we put a Scott Joplin record on the stereo. It was one of Keefer's favorites.

To the music of "Sugar Cane," we began to dance-walk around the room on the outside of our imaginary spats, twirling imaginary canes and fluttering imaginary straw hats, and rolling our eyes like an old time vaudeville team. Phil came to the doorway on his bandy legs and watched us slyly while trying to repress one of his helplessly sinister cackles behind his knobby wrist. A few seconds later, Cousin Vito stuck his horse face over Phil's shoulder and gazed at us with lunatic delight. Then Mario appeared with a broad grin on his fat face and filled in the rest of the archway.

"Heh-heh. Good boy, Keeper. Look at 'im dance!"

"You guys are good," exclaimed Mario. "Right, Cousin Vito?"

"Hey, I ain't never seen beddah–not even in Union City!"

The happy music and silly commotion drew Linda downstairs. Phil and the boys quieted down. Phil smiled and cackled and nodded in our direction, encouraging her to appreciate the spectacle we were making of ourselves. Holding the collar of her robe to her throat, she stepped cautiously into the room and smiled wanly. We pretended not to notice and kept on dancing. But we rolled our eyes a little more, and lifted our legs higher, and danced a little more on the sides of our shoes.

"What are you two goons up to?"

We didn't dare answer, we just kept dancing. Her face was glowing with a soft quizzical delight, and we didn't want to do anything that might break the spell. Keefer had all the instincts of a natural-born ham. He knew we had to keep dancing, that we shouldn't do anything that might shatter the mood. I never had to tell him anything, or show him a dance step, or anything like that. He followed my lead, knowing instinctively what to do next.

"Aren't they silly, Daddy?"

"Yeh. Heh-heh."

For a second I was tempted to bring her into the dance, but I was afraid to touch her and maybe ruin the effect the music was having. She looked so shyly happy that I didn't want to do anything to spoil it. The record ended to a round of applause and laughter. Keefer took a deep bow and went off to watch the adventures of Ultraman.

The rest of us gathered at the table, over coffee and dessert.

Linda sat next to me. I took her hand and held it, but she didn't return the pressure. I let it go, so she could use it to steady her dish, when I saw she was having trouble with her ice cream.

Phil cleared his throat.

"T'morrah, we go back to the Island."

Linda winced as if she'd been stabbed in the side. Phil kept his eyes on his ice cream. He was whipping it with his spoon, turning it into soup, which was the way he preferred to eat it. After a pause, during which she stared at him pitiably, a stare he either did not see or choose to ignore, she said quietly, "Please, Daddy. Stay a little longer. We love having you and the fellas here. Don't we, Earl?"

I said, yes we did.

"Please, Daddy?"

"Naw, we gotta get back. The business, we gotta take care of business. Then we go down to Florida for a while."

"I'll come down as soon as I'm feeling better."

"Good, good. When you come, bring Ur 'n' the lil' prince, eh?"

"Can't you stay a little longer, Daddy?"

"No-no, dahlin'. It's-ah time to go home."

Meekly she nodded her head. She looked ready to cry. Shortly afterwards, she went back upstairs. I put Keefer to bed at ten, and the rest of us played cards and drank Grappa until two in the morning. When I went up to bed, she was sound asleep.

The next morning, Phil insisted on taking us shopping at the mall before he and the boys started for the Island. He bought Keefer a creamy-colored ten-gallon cowboy hat, some leather boots, and a pair of black and white cowhide chaps, to go with his new cowboy suit.

"You come up, I gotta a ranch 'n' a pony for you."

Keefer thought this was a fine idea. He wanted to start for the Island right away. But I told him to settle down and enjoy what he had and stop being a pain. He went off to sulk in the toy store. As he walked off, I told him to meet us out front of Wanamaker's in fifteen minutes, but he didn't answer me, and, with a reassuring nod of his bony head, Cousin Vito trailed after him to make sure that he didn't get into trouble.

Phil conned me into going into a men's store with him, saying he was looking for a new hat, and then insisted on buying me a suit. Naturally he picked out the most expensive one on the rack. When I told him I didn't need a suit, he got angry and began to make a scene. He waved his arms around until I gave in and allowed the tailor to measure me. When we were finished and everything was paid for, I thanked him. He nodded coldly.

"Next time, don't be so proud."

Then he and Mario dragged Linda into a jewelry store. She kept laughing and looking back at me to see how I was taking it. They were pretending to force her through the doorway. It was all supposed to be funny and lighthearted. I could see she was excited and wanted whatever he was ready to buy her. That day it turned out to be an emerald ring set with diamond chips, really a beautiful stone. When Phil demanded the price, the clerk stuck his nose in the air and said, "That one is five thousand four hundred dollars, sir."

In his dirty overcoat and baggy pants, Phil didn't look as if he could afford a cup of coffee, much less pay for a ring with a price tag like that. He cocked his head and squinted up at the clerk.

"Ain't you got nothin' beddah?" and started counting the cash, all hundreds, out of his coat pocket. The rest of us laughed ourselves goofy at the surprised look on the clerk's face.

So that was it: beat up the doctor, throw a little money around, and head for the exits. Phil was ready to get down to business again.

CHAPTER | THREE

"Earl! Wake up!"

I woke with a horrible sense of dread in the cold and dark. Linda's sudden cry sluiced through me like an electric shock and exited with a jolt through the soles of my feet. Her face was crushed against my chest. I could hear the sleet against the windows again.

I reached over and snapped on the lamp. I lay back and held her. A shadow was beating on the ceiling above me. It opened and closed its wings like a camera lens. It took me a second to realize it was the pulse behind my eyes.

"What is it, Linda?"

"I had a terrible dream. The baby was standing at the foot of the bed, smiling at us. He was all bathed in flame, perfectly formed, outlined in fire! Oh God--it was awful!"

The small hairs on the back of my neck stood on end. I held her tightly and smoothed the thick shiny black hair back from her forehead. We lay there, holding each other tightly.

"Listen to the sleet against the windows! God, don't I hate winter!"

"You want a cup of coffee? How about I make you some coffee?"

We got out of bed and turned on the light in the hallway.

"Let's look in on Keefer."

Quietly we pushed open the door to his room until the light from the hall sprang across the foot of his bed. He was sleeping on top of his covers with his thumb in his mouth.

"Where's Bah Bear?"

"He must be on the bottom."

"Poor ol' Bah. He'll be flat as a pancake in the morning."

She put a hand to her mouth as we looked at him, lying there in his yellow pajamas on top of his bear and the covers, his dark hair mussed up and his mouth open and his wet thumb still in it.

"He's got a lot on his mind, hasn't he?"

"He's beautiful. Isn't he beautiful?"

Downstairs we ate the last of the chocolate-chip cookies.

"You think he'll mind if we eat his cookies?"

"I'll buy some more at the store. He doesn't care, so long as they keep coming."

"That's right," she said. "He's a sport about his cookies. Let's have another."

Her face tightened when she smiled. It was enough to start the tears out of her eyes again.

"It's pretty bad, isn't it?"

"Yes, it's pretty bad."

"Maybe we ought to get away. What do you think? You think a couple of weeks in the sun would help?"

"I don't know, maybe. What about Keefer?"

"We'll time it so he can stay with Phil and the boys in Florida. They'll be going down to the house in another week or so. We'll drop him off and go somewhere by ourselves."

"Maybe we ought to take him with us."

"Maybe we should get away by ourselves. He'll have a good time with them. They'll take him to the Magic Kingdom and Universal Studios. They'll spoil him rotten. He'll love every minute of it."

She picked a chocolate chip out of her cookie and put it on the end of her tongue.

"I'm not feeling very romantic."

"I know. We should wait anyway, according to your buddy, Dr. Tom. We'll go away like a couple of old friends. We're old friends, aren't we?"

"Sometimes."

We laughed.

"That's good enough, isn't it?"

"Not always," she smiled.

"Well, tonight it's good enough. I'll look into it tomorrow. Any place you want to go particularly?"

"Just so it's warm, so I can lie in the sun."

"I don't know what we can find this late. We'll find something."

"What about work?"

"It's all right. I'll work it out with Arthur."

"Maybe we shouldn't."

"Oh yes we should."

So we went away. The travel agent said that the only place in the Caribbean that wasn't booked solid was Curaçao, and so like good, obedient children we went to Curaçao.

We stayed in Willemstad in the nice hotel they'd made out of the old fort at the mouth of the harbor. The pool deck was on the roof. Sometimes I would mount the wide circular wrought-iron stairs with her after breakfast and sit in a deck chair and try to read while she sunbathed or swam languidly up and down the length of the pool. But the sun was always too bright, and after a few minutes I retreated to our room, where I could read in comfort.

We had the coffee shop and the pool virtually to ourselves. There was never anybody else around. It was the same in town. It had the uncanny emptiness of an amusement park out of season. You could sense everything had been arranged for your convenience and that the real denizens of the place were remaining discreetly in the background and would only come out of hiding after you spent your last dollar and went home. Then they would come out and cautiously have a look around. Once they were assured that the tourists were gone they would blow a whistle and have a party and real life on the island would start up again.

Sometimes we wandered around on the roof and leaned out

of the crenellations high above the waves and gazed over the limitless plain of bright water that stretched from the sheer wall of the fort out to the horizon. The ocean lay in bands of brilliant color. At the base of the wall it was an iridescent golden green. In the middle distance it became a crude semicircle of magenta. Then it cooled into an icy light-blue color that streamed outward toward the horizon, where the ocean and sky joined together without a seam.

It was all very pleasant and languid and uninspiring and yet satisfying at the same time. We weren't looking for excitement, and certainly the place had none to offer.

On the Outra Banda heights, overlooking the bay and the town, stood what had once been a small fort. Legend had it that it was once under the command of Captain Bligh. Now it was a pleasant restaurant, and we dined there several nights during our stay. Iron grilles barred the tall narrow windows and divided the twinkling lights of the harbor into grids, suggestive of a star map on the ceiling of a planetarium. Mild evening breezes streamed in the windows carrying subtle fragrances of the island. These we enjoyed, but couldn't identify. We often stopped in the middle of dinner to gaze out the tall narrow grilled window by our table at the harbor below. It made for a lovely restful scene. I looked at the moon and the dark outlines of the harbor side buildings with their Dutch façades and the glitter of moonlight on the water and wondered whether any of this was doing her any good.

Sometimes in the mornings she induced me to put my book aside and go for a walk. There was a pedestrian bridge on pontoons that was supposed to link the two sides of the harbor, but it was out of order during our visit. The thing had a three-bar railing, a humpbacked splintery wooden walkway, and metal arches overhead every few yards, encrusted with light bulbs, which made it look like a carnival ride. It was supposed to swing on a hinge like a gate. When it swung shut, people could walk across its wooden spine from one side of the harbor to the other. When it swung open, the cruise ships, the oil tankers, and the produce boats from Venezuela could swim in and out of the harbor's back rooms.

It was a wonderful proposition, but purely theoretical while we were there. The bridge was moored on the Outra Banda shore, where workmen tinkered with the outboard motor that was supposed to open and close the bridge, but they couldn't get it to work. Meanwhile, everybody rode back and forth on the ferry, or walked the long way around.

Our walks often took us by the bridge. We watched puzzled mechanics sweating over the machinery. Once a dark man we took to be the foreman stood up from his painful crouching position over the engine as we watched from the railings above the bridge. Slowly he wiped his perspiring face with a red bandanna and looked at us. He was so black we couldn't make out his features in the dazzling sunlight, but he seemed to be silently imploring us for advice. We didn't have any to give. When the man continued to stand there stubbornly, mopping his face with the bandanna and silently imploring us like that, we grew uncomfortable and decided to move on. It was funny the way he looked at us, as if we had the answers. A few days later we passed the bridge again. This time the ragamuffin mechanics were gone. Tools and small pieces of machinery lay scattered on the gray splintery planks of the walkway. We never saw the workmen again, although the next time we passed the bridge we noticed the tools and parts had disappeared.

One day we rented an orange Volkswagen Beetle through the car rental desk in the hotel lobby and circled the island. The road northwest out of Willemstad took us through parched countryside dotted with giant cactus. The car made a racket as we passed through the sun struck landscape. A huge cloud of white dust rose behind us on the road and followed us everywhere like a specter. We didn't pass any other cars outside of town. We saw only occasional signs of human habitation along the road in the shape of shabby little pastel boxlike dwellings where inevitably a few red and blue rags hung limply from a wash line in the front yard and a few scrawny chickens scratched in the dirt behind a low wire. Once we saw a goat tethered to a cactus.

We passed the moldering remains of what once had been farms built by the Dutch. The buildings with their red tile roofs and walled courtyards and cracked white plaster walls sat in the dust and silence. The broken windows were shuttered and the doors boarded over. We looked at the cactus and the arid land and wondered what the Dutch could have grown here to warrant building such estates, which you could see must have been lovely at one time. Whatever had caused them to settle here had obviously ended in disaster.

We stopped for lunch at the restaurant at Westpunt, a clearing with a few houses on the western tip of the island. We were the only customers in the place. As soon as the young girl served the food, she disappeared. I wanted another beer, but she never came back. When it came time to pay the bill I went to the bar and shouted into the open doorway of the kitchen. I could hear some people murmuring somewhere out of sight. After a time they stopped talking and seemed to listen thoughtfully. Eventually a stout middle-aged man with a gray Fu Manchu mustache came into view and collected the money.

When we got back to Willemstad that afternoon, I was confused by the signs and the novelty of the traffic after traveling through the empty countryside, and kept forgetting to drive on the left side of the road. All the rental cars on the island were orange so the natives could take appropriate evasive measures. I drove down a one-way street for several blocks before I realized what I was doing. In the meantime, the carts and wagons and other cars streamed past us unperturbed.

One day, walking along a chalky road on the Outra Banda, we found ourselves in the middle of a festival that materialized out of nowhere. The music was provided by a few horns and many steel drums. A crowd of dancing islanders surged around us. Dark little children dressed in bright yellow feathery chicken costumes, their heads peeping out below orange bills, peered solemnly ahead in the morning sunlight as they were pulled along on floats, surrounded by dancers and musicians.

"What's going on?" I asked some of the people passing by. But they were either oblivious or understood only Papiamento, and danced around us as if we were posts in the roadway.

"Is today a holiday?" I asked a man with bloodshot eyes and grizzled hair. But the man, like everybody else, appeared not to hear me.

The tide of people rose around us. We were submerged in the crowd and the noise. The fluty music and metallic drum beats reached a crescendo. The solemn feathered children passed by on the floats with great dignity. Then the sea of people and the music and the children got up like chickens suddenly receded and left us standing by ourselves like so much flotsam swirling in the chalky dust at the edge of the road. The beautiful solemn children, their yellow feathers turned and flapping in the breeze, shrank away in the distance. The music grew tremulous and weak on the wind and then died away. White sand, fine as lime dust, blew across the crumbling roadway as we watched the procession crest a hill and disappear from view. It was beautiful, maybe the best thing that happened to us while we were there. Neither of us understood what it was about, and that was a good thing because it was simply beautiful, the drums, the singing and the dancing and the commotion over the children dressed as chickens, and we were afraid any attempt to explain its meaning would have ruined it.

Our room overlooked the ocean. Some nights we sat out on the balcony after dinner and had a drink. Usually we put in a call to Pompano Beach to find out how Keefer was getting along. He was always getting along fine, which disappointed us a little. We thought it would be nice if he missed us, but he didn't seem to. Nevertheless it made her feel better to talk to him every night.

"I know I'm silly. Do you think I'm silly?"

"No, you're not silly. Let's call, if it'll put your mind at ease."

"Geez, he doesn't even miss us, does he?"

"He doesn't seem to."

"The little brat. Daddy and the fellas are spoiling him rotten."

"I told you he'd love it."

She had trouble sleeping at first, so we each took one of the double beds. Things seemed to be going pretty well. I had explained the situation to Arthur, and he was very understanding, even though my absence meant a lot of extra work for him. But he wanted me to go. He told me to go away and stay away for as long as it took. I decided we'd stay on as long as she wanted to. I didn't think it would be too long. But I thought it would be nice to let her bring up the subject of going home first. When she was ready, she would let me know.

She got into the habit of rising early and going up to the pool by herself for a swim. By the time she got back, I was usually up and shaved and showered and ready to take her to breakfast. One morning, no different from several others, I woke to find her bed empty as usual. I walked into the bathroom without giving it a thought and found her pale and naked, staring at herself in the bathroom mirror. Tears were streaming out of her wide dark eyes.

"Linda, what's wrong?"

"I don't know. I feel sad."

She covered her face, made an effort at the same time to hide her breasts with her forearms. I picked her robe off the floor and put it over her shoulders. With a grateful look, she wriggled into the heavy white terry cloth and tightened the belt about her waist.

"Sorry to be such a wet blanket."

"It's okay. I'm sorry I walked in on you. I thought you were at the pool. Aren't you having a good time? I thought you were having a good time."

"I miss Keefer."

"I know you do. You want to go home?"

"I want to go down to Florida with Daddy and Mario. I want to stay with them for a while. Can I?"

She tightened her belt again and smiled at me uncertainly.

"What about his schooling?"

"I can enroll him down there for a few months."

I looked at the floor.

"I don't think I can stand to be at home this winter. I want to be somewhere where it's warm. Is it okay?"

"Jesus, Linda. I wish you'd get over this. This is no way to live."

"I know, I'm sorry. I can't help it."

She looked at me in the mirror. She was miserable about it, but that's the way she felt. She was still holding the ends of the belt in her hands, even though she was finished with it.

"I need some time for myself. Please don't get mad at me."

"I'm not mad, I wish you'd get over it. If you want to go down there, it's all right with me. How long do you plan to stay?"

"I don't know."

"Well it's fine with me."

"Don't be mad."

"I'm not mad. A little disappointed, maybe, but not mad."

Her eyes were glittering with tears again as she looked at me in the mirror.

"I still think about the baby."

"I know you do."

"I miss him. Isn't that silly?"

"No, it's not silly."

"Some people would say he was never really alive. I never got to hold him in my arms or anything. But I miss him awful."

"Maybe you'd better not talk about it. It makes it worse."

"He was such a beautiful baby. It's almost as bad as if we'd lost Keefer–"

"Please don't bring Keefer's name into it."

"You think it's bad luck?"

"I don't know what it is, but don't do it."

"I'm sorry."

"It's all right. You want me to get you some tissues?"

"Sometimes I think God took the baby away because I said I

didn't want him. When I first found out, I said I didn't want to get fat again. I said one kid was enough. I even talked about getting an abortion. You remember? You think that's what happened?"

"Don't be ridiculous."

"That's right. Don't be ridiculous. He won't hurt Keefer, don't worry."

"I'm not worried."

"I'm sorry, I brought his name into it again."

"It's all right. Let's get off this subject. Let's go have some breakfast. Then I'll see about the tickets. Is that what you want?"

"Yes. How about tomorrow?"

"Sure. Why not?"

It'll be a relief to be alone, I thought. It'll be a relief to come home and not have to look at her. It'll be nice to come home to an empty house and not have to contend with her problems. I can eat out in restaurants and read the papers. I can get a lot of extra work done. Maybe it'll work out for everybody. We got dressed and went down and had breakfast. Afterwards I took care of the tickets, and the next morning we got out of there.

When we got home, we discovered an anti-abortionist group nobody ever heard of had planted a bomb under Dr. Monaghan's Toyota, immolating the old man where he sat. The heat from the explosion was so intense it fused his hand bones to the steering wheel. An anonymous tip led the authorities to the leader of the group, a man named John Scaramucci, an unemployed construction worker with a history of drug abuse and long periods of homelessness. They found the bomb making materials in his one-room apartment and his fingerprints on the trunk lid of Monaghan's car. In court, a cellmate testified that Scaramucci had confessed that he'd done the crime because, "killing babies was against God's law, and God's law is higher than man's law."

His sister, the only surviving member of his family, was a witness for the defense. "John was not right in his head ever since Viet Nam," she said. "He hears voices telling him to do things but, even if a voice told him to do it, I don't think he would do a thing like that. No, I don't think so."

The poor woman's testimony unintentionally sealed her brother's fate. The jury was out less than an hour before returning a guilty verdict. His court appointed attorney appealed, claiming that Scaramucci was innocent by reason of insanity, but the appeal was denied. Scaramucci went to the electric chair, still raving that he was innocent.

"It's terrible what he did to that poor old man," Linda said. "I'm glad they gave him the chair. But, you know, when you go around killing babies, you're asking for big trouble."

Gino, the mechanic, flashed into the soft matter that passes for my brain when she said that, but in an earlier conversation she'd told me that Gino had gone back to Italy.

"He had to go back. His mother is not well."

Ah. *La famiglia*. I should have known.

CHAPTER | FOUR

I was in Atlanta on business during the first week in May. After it was finished, I made arrangements to fly down to Fort Lauderdale and spend a long weekend in Pompano Beach. It was a soft warm tropical night when I arrived, the breeze ruffled my hair and searched the pockets of my flapping suit jacket as I crossed the tarmac. Cousin Vito was waiting for me by the gate. He was standing in the middle of a stumpy group of Cuban women. His head and long neck stood out above them like a dried apple on a stick.

As always, he greeted me with barely contained zany elation, like a young hunting dog out in the field for the first time. He punched me repeatedly in the seam between shoulder and chest where the arm bone is closest to the surface, giving his knuckles a little corkscrew twist at the end each time, and asked me over and over again how I was. Theses subclavian punches hurt and put a little edge on my smile. Besides punching me and asking how I was, he never knew what else to do or say to me, although he liked me a lot. Despite my protestations, he insisted on carrying my bag to the car for me. He was forty years older than I was, but he insisted, and I let him, rather then hurt his feelings.

When I got to the house, Keefer was already in bed. Someone had told Mario that he made the best margaritas in southern Florida. He was throwing a little party in the courtyard by the pool to further his reputation as a great drink mixer. Linda held her drink away, so she wouldn't spill it, and pressed her cheek against mine in a sort of distracted greeting full of bird cries of delight. She led me around by the hand and introduced me to everyone. She was wearing a gray silk blouse and an off-white nubbly shantung skirt, and her shiny black hair was done up in a kind of geisha style that was very attractive. Her rings threw off sparks as she fluttered her hands about during the animated introductions she was conducting on my behalf.

"And *guess* who this is! This is Earl! My *husband!* I told y'all I had one!"

"Y'all?" I whispered. "What have you been doing? Reading *Gone with the Wind*?"

She laughed and pressed her hand to the gold medallions glinting in the soft shadows at the opening of her blouse. The silver and gold hoop bracelets on her slender arms clinked together expensively.

"Oh my God! Did I really say that? Marvin, have you met my husband? I actually do have one, you know."

The lighted pool was neon blue, like a giant Paraiba tourmaline. She walked me around to the other side, where Phil, looking uncomfortable in a tie and dinner jacket, stood in conclave with some of the guests, with a finger inside his shirt collar in order to give himself some breathing room. In his other hand, he waved a cigar with a red-hot coal at the end of it. The men had their heads together, standing as close to him as they dared to, with that hot cigar in his hand. Phil darted glances at his attendant circle out of the sides of his glittery narrow eyes. He was relating some inanity with the air of confiding a valuable secret. He was speaking in a gravelly stage whisper that could be heard ten feet away.

Apparently we came up as he delivered the punch line. They began to laugh as the circle broke apart to welcome us. One man, with white hair and shiny smooth pink skin, threw back his cottony little goatee and showed us the fat underside of his throbbing throat as he crowed like a rooster. Phil shouldered him aside and gave me an embrace, ending with a little arm's-length shake by the shoulders.

"Ur! Where you been? I try to call 'n' tell you to come down last week! Whaddya do? Makin' money for Uncle Sam?"

He was smiling but his cheeks were mottled with a hot looking flush. His eyes were glassy and he looked tired. He didn't like parties, but he put up with them for the sake of Linda and Mario. They liked to entertain when they were in Florida.

He was glad to see me, but I could tell he was struggling to keep from giving me hell for not coming down more often. He took me by the arm and turned me around.

"See this good-looking man? He's ah my son-in-law. Linda's husband. He's a smart boy, too, eh? Too busy workin' all the time to come see us. Heh-heh."

The jovial man with the goatee turned out to be a federal judge. The short thin dark nervous fellow, who had stepped back into the shadows at our approach and then stepped back into the light again when Phil introduced us, fixed us with a benign expression of penetrating calculation, like that of a savvy old tobacco merchant or cotton broker. His complexion was the sallow color of someone who had worked out of doors for years and now was forced to spend all his time inside. He was angular and sharp-edged, like a piece of sculpture soldered together with steel rods and snippets of tin. He owned orange groves and said he was thinking of buying a newspaper.

Vinny Palumbo was also among Phil's poolside circle of conspirators. He was down to attend to some complicated piece of family business having to do with real estate. He seemed surprised at first, and then inordinately pleased, to see me. He shook my hand and put his arm around me and told me what a long time it had been. I didn't remember that we'd ever been that friendly.

"How's your brother?"

He acted surprised that I remembered he had one. Everything seemed to catch him off balance.

"Oh, yeah. Fine, thanks. He had a cyst so bad he couldn't sit down. He's better now."

He gave Linda a kiss on the cheek and held her by the hands as if ready to skip down the length of poolside with her.

"You're looking very elegant tonight."

She bobbed in a mock curtsy.

"Well thank you very much, kind sir."

I met the new neighbors over by the bar, where Cousin Vito and Mario were holding court. Their names were Evita and Armando Goodman. They professed to be dear friends of Linda's.

"What a darling wife you have!"

"Yes! She is so vibrant!"

They said I would never know how delighted they were to meet me at last. Armando was short and tense and prone to sudden outbursts of false laughter. He had short curly black hair. A luxuriant mustache swept along his cheekbones but didn't quite connect with his sideburns. He stood by his wife's side with the air of a boy going through the agonies of puberty. She was an artificial but tastefully done blond. She had an exotic Mayan cast to her face, with full lips and a rather fleshy nose and almond-shaped eyes, which she had exaggerated with her eyeliner. She was not pretty in the conventional sense, but she was very striking. She was tall and stood very straight and showed off a lovely pair of breasts. I had the feeling she never forgot where they were. She did her best to make sure that Armando and I didn't either, by contriving to move her torso constantly as she talked, so we could appreciate the architecture from every angle. Armando was just tall enough so that if he stood on tippytoe, he could have hooked his nose in her cleavage.

We were standing by the bar. Armando happened to mention that he had never had a margarita. His family owned vineyards in Chile, he said, and he drank only wine, principally the vintage made and bottled by his family. Mario immediately took away his wineglass and insisted on fixing Armando one of his specialities. At first Armando protested. He held up the palms of his hands, buried his chin in his collar, and shook his head in protest.

"No, no, my friend. I couldn't possibly."

"Try one," said Evita. "Don't be such a piss all your life."

Armando took a cautious sip. He cocked his head and looked

at his glass in surprise as if it had a false bottom or a trick compartment.

"Delightful," he said.

He tossed off the rest of it and smiled at us.

"*Magnifico,* my friend. That was like a short vacation."

"Careful," I said. "Those are sneaky."

I think he had two more. Within fifteen minutes he was asleep on the floor at the foot of his wife's chair. She reached down and patted his head.

"Poor Armando's exhausted. The experiment was too much for him."

She was good-natured about it. After a while, she stepped over him and left him lying there on the tile floor and came over to me.

"Armando's liable to have a stiff neck in the morning."

"Never mind about Armando, darling. Linda didn't tell us you were such a handsome man. She said you used to be a naughty little boy. You climbed all over the outside of your house at night and spied in the windows to catch your parents making love. Is this true?"

"No. Not much of it. But I did climb on the house. It was sort of my jungle gym."

"Ah, now we're getting someplace! And did you spy on your poor mommy and poppy like that?"

"Yes, but not in the way you mean."

"*Caramba!* You were a naughty boy! And what are you now?"

"Pardon me?"

"I said, what are you now? Did you grow up to be a naughty man? Or are you tame, like my sweet Armando, who has two drinks and curls up and sleeps like a big dog at my feet?"

Linda came and rescued me at that point.

"I promise to bring him right back, Evita."

She took me by the hand and started to lead me away.

"I want him to see Keefer. He looks so cute in his bed tonight."

As we went upstairs I said, "I think she wanted to know if my monkey was at home."

"Did it flatter you? She likes to break in all the new men."

"Well anyway, thanks for the rescue."

"Do you think she's attractive?"

"Attractive? I suppose so. She has a sort of a Barrymore profile."

Linda snorted. "You mean you could use her nose for a bottle opener."

"Yes, she'd be handy on picnics."

She turned and smiled.

"Don't agree with me so fast. It makes you sound guilty."

I fell into her like a meteor being pulled into the sun. She tasted sweet as a tangerine. I pushed up her dress and pulled down her panties, and not six feet from Keefer's door, we made love against the wall. Or rather we started against the wall. Slowly we slid down and ended in a tangle on the floor.

"Don't roll on me with all that jewelry. You're liable to give me contusions and puncture wounds."

"Stop it. You're always so damned silly when you're supposed to be serious."

She covered her mouth with both her hands to keep the sounds from coming out. "Shh-shh!" I whispered in her ear. I think we made a lot of noise. We were very excited. It actually hurt my plumbing a little bit, it had been so long. Afterwards I said, "I hope you took your PEP pill today."

"My pep pill?"

"Yes, that stands for your Prevent Eventual People Pill."

"Yes, I took it okay. I always take it now."

"I hope you haven't had any special reason to take it lately."

"No, I haven't. Not really."

"Not really?"

"I can't say I haven't been tempted. Vinny's been down here on business a couple of times."

"Oh no. Not that greaseball. Were you able to restrain yourself?"

"Would you forgive me if I hadn't?"

"Just say, 'Yes, I was able to restrain myself.'"

"Okay. Yes, I was able to restrain myself."

She thought for a moment.

"The last time I did anything like that was when Arthur and I had a little go of it."

"Really? When did this happen?"

"Oh, years ago. We were still in college. When your father was sick and you went home. Remember? Arthur offered to console me."

"Jesus. My friend, Arthur. Did you let him?"

"Almost. Close enough to feel guilty about it. Arthur said he'd die if I didn't let him."

"But you didn't."

"No. I shook him until he went off in his pants like a bottle of soda pop."

She laughed.

"I think I ruined half a dozen pair of slacks for him. I used to call him old sticky pockets. How is he, anyway?"

"Just the same. He's got some new tootsie on the string. She lets him tie her to the bed with his neckties. He takes snapshots of her. He showed me some at the racquet club the other day."

"God, he's weird."

"He keeps his tennis duds and a change of clothes at her place. She takes his tennis shirt to bed with her when he's not there. She says she loves the smell of his body. It really turns her on. She takes the shirt to bed with her so she can smell him in the dark and pretend he's there with her. Arthur was very proud of this when he told me."

"I'll bet he was."

"I asked him if he still had his bicycle. He got that silly little crease between his eyebrows. 'What's that got to do with it?' he said. 'Well,' I said, 'you could save some money and give her the seat for Christmas.'"

"What did he say?"

"He laughed like hell."

We lay there and laughed together on the floor.

"Daddy? Is that you?"

For a moment we were stunned.

"Just a minute, son. We'll be right in."

We scrambled to our feet and straightened our clothes. Linda shoved her panties down the front of her dress. Her mouth quickly skated over my face. In the process she pinched my lower lip with her tiny white teeth until my eyes watered. Then she slipped off to the bathroom and I went in to see him.

He was so happy to see me. "Dad! Dad!" he kept saying as if he couldn't believe it. He stood up on the bed and hugged me. I settled him down again. Linda came in and stood by the doorway and with her arms folded and watched us, with the faint wick of a smile on her face. I made Bah Bear do a dance on his chest and sing a few lines of "Don Gato":

"Oh, Senor Don Gato was a cat,

On a high red roof Don Gato sat--"

Out in the hallway she whispered, "You think he heard us?"

"I don't think so."

As we got to the top of the stairs, I heard him cry out jubilantly.

"Dad!"

"What is it, son?"

"How do you get love out of your body?"

We looked at each other.

"I don't know, son. How?"

"By kissing!"

"Okay, son. Settle down now and go to sleep."

We started down the stairs.

"I think he heard us."

"Not a chance," I said.

CHAPTER | FIVE

How do you get love out of your body? Sometimes you use it all up, Keefer, and you try to replenish it by doing something stupid. Either one of us might have been caught in the act of sabotaging our faux marriage. It was even possible that Linda had already had her go at repletion under the Florida palm fronds with Vinny Palumbo, or the tan guy with the orange groves, or maybe she had bucked up poor Armando out of the goodness of her heart, but regardless I was always the bigger fool and the more likely one to be caught. They say that men are the more unforgiving, but those sages hadn't met Linda. I know what I'm doing here. I'm spreading the blame around. Even now, these many years later, I can't stand to take it alone.

During the last weekend in June, The National Association for Hardware Dealers met in Atlantic City. We'd done a lot of work for them over the years. I went down to talk to the executive committee about doing some more. At one of the cocktail parties, I met a pleasant young woman from Thailand. She told me that she now lived in Houston, Texas. I believe she worked in some capacity for the hardware association down there, but I never really got that straight. Much of the time it was hard for me to understand what she was saying. She spoke in many different musical registers in order to make up for her difficulties with the language. When I told her my name was Earl, she tilted her little cat-shaped face, pursed her lips, and blew it back to me in two notes as through a bamboo flute.

"Er-roo?"

I was utterly charmed.

"Er-roo? Is'n tha awry?"

It certainly was. It always had been awry. I wanted something better, something altogether my own, instead of the leftover part of Ray's name. But this little Thai woman, in the low-cut organdy cocktail dress, with the lovely freckles on her bosom, made my hand-me-down name as suitable-sounding to my ears as ever it had been, by immediately transfiguring it into the sweet fluty idiom that the mourning doves in the trees around my house used for calling to each other in the dark treetops.

Her name was Yingluck, close enough to "bad luck" to be an omen, but I was utterly charmed and ready to make a fool of myself. I won't make a long story of it. I took her to dinner. After much conversation and wine, I took her to bed. We woke early in the morning. Both of us wanted to prolong our pleasant time together. It was one of those twenty-four hour love affairs that make you feel as though you're in the movies. We knew it wasn't real. But it was so nice neither of us wanted to end it right away. It was pleasant to be in the company of a woman who didn't want to get away from me as soon as she could. I proposed we put on our swimsuits and go out and wade in the ocean. We could hold hands and feel the delicious chill of sea air and salt water on our bodies. We could watch the day strengthen on the beach for a few minutes. Then we would come back and have breakfast in my room. She went to her room to put on her bathing suit. I was to meet her in the lobby in fifteen minutes. It gave me enough time to change and call home.

The day before, I had told Linda that I might be able to make it home that night. I said I couldn't be sure. It depended on business—funny business as it turned out. She said in that case she wouldn't look for me. That's the way we'd left it. I thought I'd better check in with her again.

"So it ran longer than you expected."

"Everybody talks too much at these meetings. We have another one this morning. I ought to be out of here by noon."

"Drive carefully."

"Thanks, I will."

I met Yingluck in the lobby and shortly thereafter we were up to our necks in the ocean, bobbing up and down on the waves. She was only a little thing, but she had a beautiful body. I took her out where we could have some privacy. She had to dog paddle to keep her chin above water. She took off the bottom of her suit and I took off my trunks and handed them to her. The water was cold; I smoothed my hands against her snowy thighs and slipped my fingers inside her. Despite the frigid water I felt myself getting hard. Her legs levitated buoyantly. She locked her feet around the small of my back. Her head went back. She closed her eyes and smiled as her long black hair spread in S-curves on the water. I drew her closer. I tried to get her seated on me. Even though I was partly anesthetized, we managed it after a while. It wasn't much fun at first. I danced back against the tide and pulled her closer. Gradually everything began to improve.

Over her shoulder I saw a tow-headed boy on a yellow inner tube paddling towards us through the rise and fall of the gentle swell. I stopped. When I did, she raised her head out of the water to see what the matter was.

"Oh-oh. What we do now, Er-roo?"

"Nothing to worry about. It's just a kid."

"Quick now! Bettah tacky you pahts!"

She handed them to me in an underwater pass.

"Bettah I get in mine too!"

She struggled like a puppy in my arms, but the water was too deep for her.

"Wait a minute. He'll go away. Then I'll get you in a little closer and you'll be able to get them on all right."

"Hokay."

Our heads bobbed like seabirds above the saw-toothed waves. We watched the kid methodically paddle towards us, looking up urgently between seas, to see if we were still there. I thought we were perfectly safe. The water was loaded with sediment and fairly opaque. But she lowered herself a few more inches into the water, until it slopped greedily about her chin and lips. Doggedly the kid paddled closer. He kept looking at us as if he had something important to tell us, if only he could get close enough. He had water goggles on, sort of like the kind the old-time aviators wore, with round raised lenses framed in bottle-cap metal and fixed in a strap of black rubber with a buckle at the back of his head.

I let him get within a few yards.

"Hello, son."

"Hullo."

He looked at me gravely. I thought he looked disappointed, as if we weren't the people he thought we were.

"Kind of deep out here for you isn't it?"

He decided not to answer this. He gave Yingluck a long last look, rotated his inner tube, and sulkily began paddling for shore.

"Er-roo?"

"Yes?"

"Bahd news."

"What's wrong?"

"I think I lose my pahts."

"You lost your pants?"

"I get ah-fraid when little boy come. I try get in. But ah-drop in watah."

"I'm sure they're around here somewhere. Let me get you in closer to shore where you can stand up. I'll put my trunks on and look for them."

"Hokay."

I felt around on the bottom with my feet. I looked all around, thinking they might be floating on the surface. I dove several times. I covered a pretty big area. I came up with a handful of kelp once, but no suit.

"Oh boy. Plenty trouble now. What we do, Er-roo?"

"I'll go up to the room and get my robe. I'll be back in a minute."

"I sorry, Er-roo. You don't like me now, I bet."

"I like you fine. It'll give us something to giggle about at breakfast. You stay here. I'll be right back."

"Hokay. Er-roo?"

"What?"

"I trusteen you."

I laughed, "Don't worry, I won't leave you out here without your pants."

"You bettah not!"

I waved when I got to the tunnel leading under the boardwalk to the hotel. She was just a dot in the surf. More people were on the beach, more of them in the water, but she was easy to find. She didn't wave back. I'm sure she didn't see me. She was bobbing in the waves a little off to the left of the lifeguard tower which lined up with the entrance to the tunnel where I was standing.

When I got to my room, I had trouble with my key. I fiddled with it until I lost my temper and began to swear. I was about to go in search of the chambermaid when the lock finally relented. I got the robe out of the closet and hurried back to the elevators. They were madding slow. It seemed like a long time, but really only ten minutes or so had passed since I had left her in the surf.

When I reached the hotel's sunny gardens I broke into a trot, passing with hollow footfalls through the cold dark tunnel out onto the warm sand. More people were in the water now. The surf had picked up in the few minutes I was gone. I looked around for her, but I didn't see her. Several bathers were in the surf in the same vicinity where she should have been, and I thought maybe I just hadn't spotted her yet. I ran down to the edge of the water. I cupped a hand over my eyes against the sun. I looked back to make sure I was lined up with the right chair. It was number three, the right one.

I draped the robe over my shoulders and waded out into the surf about waist-deep. Kids and some older people were milling around in the water obstructing my view. I began to feel a tinge of panic. I looked around for the boy with the yellow inner tube. Maybe he would know where she was. But I couldn't find him. I walked up and down the length of the beach. I went into the water in line with every lifeguard's chair to make sure I hadn't gotten the number wrong. Finally I went to the lifeguard.

"Pardon me," I said in a ridiculously polite voice to cover my panic. "I'm looking for a young lady. An oriental? Kind of short. She was standing in the water a few minutes ago. You didn't happen to see her come out, did you?"

"I don't keep track of the individuals, sir. We gotta keep the whole picture in front of us, you know? There's a pretty good riptide out there this morning."

I pointed, "She was supposed to wait for me right there."

"Maybe she got tired of waitin'."

"I don't' think so. See, she didn't have any pants on."

He stood up and blew his whistle.

"Hey, Gerald!"

He gestured to an older, patchily tanned man on the porch of the lifeguard shack up the beach. Gerald immediately started down off the porch toward us.

"You gotta talk to Gerald. He handles the complicated ones."

I told my story to Gerald. His blue eyes twinkled tolerantly as I went through it. At the end he smiled as if he had just gotten the joke.

"She probably didn't lose them. She's back in her room right now having a good laugh."

"No, Gerald. She lost them all right."

"How do you know for sure?"

"Because we were fooling around."

"Fooling around?"

"Yes. Fooling around. You understand what I mean, Gerald?"

He blinked.

"Oh yeah, right. Now I get it."

"She got nervous when a little boy came too close. That's when she dropped them."

"Maybe she found them when you went off."

"I don't think so. Do you?"

Gerald scratched his whiskers.

"Maybe we better talk to Mackey."

"Who's Mackey?"

"He's the cop on the beach this morning. You sure of this story?"

"It really happened, Gerald."

"Okay," he said with a sigh. "Let's go see Mackey."

We found Mackey sitting in a black-and-white cruiser further up the beach. Gerald left me seated in the back, and with evident relief returned to his shack above the sand. Mackey heard my story through the screen that separated the front and back seats of his patrol car, listening to me with his head cocked to one side like a priest hearing a confession. Then he said we had to go over to the station and tell Father Moriarty my sins. That would be Sergeant Moriarty. Apparently I was going to have to work my way up to the governor before I could get anybody to do anything about the poor woman I'd left to drown in the surf.

The station was three blocks back from the beach. After I finished telling Moriarty the story, he wanted to hear it again. It was hard to know whether he was digging for facts or enjoying my discomfort. He had gray hairs bristling out of his big honker of a nose and little blue pebbles for eyes, all of which did not endear him to me.

"You say she was registered in the same hotel?"

"I think so."

"You sure she wasn't a prostitute?"

"No, no. I told you before. There was no money involved."

"But you bought her dinner?"

"Yes, I bought her dinner and a few drinks. That was it."

"And then you took her back to your room?"

"Yes."

"And then what happened?"

"Look, do I have to go through all this again? I was supposed to leave this morning. My wife will be worried."

"Would you like to give her a call?"

"What I would like is to get out of here."

Moriarty pursed his lips thoughtfully.

"You didn't hurt this girl, did you, Mr. Bogwell?"

He was giving me his professional deadpan look. I suppose he'd learned it at the police academy.

"I came to you, remember? I didn't hurt her. If I had, do you think I would come to you?"

"Some people do, sir."

"Well, I'm not one of them. May I go back to my hotel now? I've really got to get home."

He offered to have Mackey drive me back to the hotel, but I said I'd rather walk. I didn't want to pull up in front of the hotel in a cop car, where some of my potential clients might be waiting for a taxi to take them to the airport. How would that look? Moriarty said they would "look into the matter," by which I suppose he meant they would wait until a body washed up on the beach. When I got to my room, I called Linda. It was after two o'clock. I explained I'd been delayed because a woman had disappeared in the surf.

"You? Why are you involved?"

"Because I saw it. One second she was there, the next she was gone. The lifeguards didn't see anything. I was the only one. I just finished telling my story to the cops."

"You sound shaken."

"I am shaken. I'll be out of here as soon as I can check out and get the car out of valet parking."

I drove across the marshlands toward Philadelphia. I got on the turnpike and started west through the rolling countryside. The sight of the stone farmhouses and the dip and rise of white board fences along the edges of the neat green fields and the pretty sight of sleek horses with nicely curried manes and fat haunches in the pastures helped a little to smooth me down. The long drive home gave me plenty of time to think about it. I couldn't get it out of my mind. When you have breath enough left to think the worst has happened, you can be sure it hasn't. But that morning I could think only that I had caused the death of a woman, and I couldn't imagine anything worse ever befalling me.

You didn't hurt this, girl, did you, Mr. Bogwell?

I did, officer. But nothing you can do will ever be punishment enough. I was ready for a life sentence of regret.

When I got home, Linda wanted to know the details. She gave me a little time first. I went upstairs and took a shower and put on some clean clothes. But when I came downstairs and the three of us sat down in the kitchen to a dinner of chicken and waffles, one of Keefer's favorite meals, she wanted to know all about it. I could see she had her antennae up. She had that curiously calm manner that some women affect when they suspect their husbands of funny business. I tried to get out of telling her. I felt awful. I didn't want to talk about it. The other thing was, I didn't want to have to lie through my teeth.

"You really think this a topic for the dinner table?"

"I'm interested to know what happened."

Keefer was sucked in by this, wanting to know the grisly details.

"You really saw someone drownded? Stevie Dietz saw a police diver pull a lady out of the river. He said an eel wiggled out of a hole in her stomach and jumped into the water."

"Keefer! That's enough of that talk."

"I'm only saying what Stevie said."

"Well, can it. I don't like it."

"Right. Put a lid on it, Keef. You know how squeamish your father is."

"Geez. Other people get to say anything they want around here. I don't know why I can't."

"Because you're a very short person. When you get taller, you can say what you want."

She turned back to me.

"What happened?"

There was no getting out of it.

I'd gone down for a swim. I noticed this oriental woman in

the surf. I took notice of her because she was so short. A wave nearly knocked me over. When I looked back, she was gone. She couldn't have gotten out of the water that fast. When I couldn't find her, I went to the lifeguard, then to the cops. That was it. That was my story.

Linda lit a cigarette and blew the smoke down the front of her blouse. She looked up at me and picked a piece of tobacco off her tongue.

"Was she pretty?"

"What kind of a question is that? I see a woman drown. And you want to know if she was pretty?"

She picked up her plate of chicken and waffles and hit me with it.

"Have some more," she pushed my plate off the table. It landed upside down in my lap.

"Fill up," she said. "Because it's your last meal in this house."

"Hey, you guys," Keefer's eyes were going fast back and forth between us as if watching a tennis match.

"You fucked her, didn't you?"

"Linda, what the hell-"

"You fucked her. She called here an hour ago. She said she'd tried to reach you at your hotel. But you'd checked out. Something about some friends coming along. Finding her. I couldn't understand half of what she said. She talked like goddam Charlie Chan. 'I so solly. I no know he mahrried.' I said, forget it. Go have a fortune cookie."

"Keefer, you better go out and play."

"No. Let him stay. Let him find out what a prick his father is. Going out of town on business trips. Fucking everybody he can lay his hands on."

"Don't talk that way in front of him."

"I'll talk any goddam way I please. Here, have some syrup on your waffles."

She started to pour the pitcher of syrup into my lap. I took it away from her. She reached around and grabbed the telephone book off the counter and smacked me alongside the head with it. I grabbed her by the front of the blouse and picked her up out of her seat and drove her against the kitchen wall.

"Don't hurt her, Dad!"

He had a piece of waffle on his fork. His face was streaming with tears. It was all scrunched up like a little old man's. Her eyes darted from side to side, looking into mine. Excited, as if dealing with a dangerous and unpredictable lover.

"Go ahead, hit me. I'll tell Daddy. He'll goddam have you killed. If he won't, I will."

I turned her around and grabbed her by the scruff of the neck and the seat of her pants and ran her out of the kitchen into the dining room. I gave her a shove and let go. She stumbled against the table and fell down on the rug. I went back into the kitchen.

"Get out!"

I heard a crash. She'd pulled the tablecloth off the table and a vase of flowers came down with it.

"Get out! Get out!"

Keefer sat there with his fork in the air staring at me. I extracted a piece of chicken from the placket of my shirt and set it on the table. I could hear her screaming and tearing the drapes down at the dining-room windows.

"I've got to go, son."

"Why's she so mad? What did you do?"

"Listen, Keefer. No matter what happens, I want you to remember that I love you."

"Are you going?"

I gave him a kiss on the top of his head.

"I'll see you in a couple of days."

Linda came back into the room and swept the dishes off the drainboard by the kitchen sink. I started for the door.

Keefer cried out, "Dad!"

Just that one syllable, in fright and bewilderment. It nearly broke my heart but for everybody's sake, I thought I'd better keep moving.

CHAPTER | SIX

A few weeks later, Phil called me. When I picked up the receiver, he was already in the middle of some apoplectic rampage that sounded as if it had been going on for ten minutes. I had no idea what he was saying, or whether he was shouting at me or to someone in the background, like Mario or Cousin Vito. The only thing I knew for sure was that it was Phil. I would have recognized his voice anywhere. I decided to interrupt, so he'd know I was on the line. We hadn't established that yet.

"Hello?"

Either he ignored this or didn't hear it. He kept on with his tirade, half in English, half in Italian. Gradually I understood that all the shouting was about me and he was telling me to go home.

"Go home! What's your son gonna do for a fahdah? Eh? Go home! Listen to me! I'm ah sick man! Don't aggravate me like dis!"

"She kicked me out, Phil."

"Whaddayou talkin' about! Are you a man or whaddayou? Go home! What are you trying to do--kill me?"

"Believe me, Phil–"

"Goddam you! Listen to me! I love you like a son, you son of a bitch! Better than that *stupido* God gave me! I don't talk to hear myself! Go home! Before I break you legs, you son of a pig! I beat you with a stick like a dog! I flatten your head so I can play checkers on it! I–"

"Phil, don't. You'll have a stroke."

"I'mah sick. Sick! You hear me? I'mah ol' man. Don't do dis

to me!"

"I'm sorry Phil–"

"Go home!" he shouted and slammed down the receiver.

I expected him on my doorstep the next morning. Maybe he'd be holding Linda by the ear with one hand and Keefer by the other. He would smile his crocodile smile until his head seemed in danger of falling off his shoulders and rolling to a stop on my doormat. He would talk fast. He would shower money around like confetti.

Whatsamaddah? holding Linda out by her ear. *You don't like no more? What if I put a pliers on you fingers? All them back bones? I have Gino break 'em like popcorn! Better yet, take a vacation! I send you to Bermudah! Hawaii! Sicily! Eh? You wanna go to Sicily? Mario, Cousin Vito, we take care of Keeper. Two weeks, good as new! A coupla lovebirds again, eh? Eh? Maybe you make two-tree babies this time! I give 'em all cowboy suits 'n' lil' ponies to ride! Then everybody's-ah happy! Every ting good again, eh?*

He would follow this speech with a gravelly laugh. It would tumble around in his chest until it activated his emphysema, forcing him to stop mixing threats with bribes and concentrate on spitting into his handkerchief. But he never showed up.

I checked into a different hotel every night for two weeks. Every morning, I check the parking lot for goons and looked under my car for bombs. I had the hood up one morning when a young man approached and ask if he could be of help.

"No! Get away!"

My nerves were shredded. Linda had lawyered up right away and wouldn't let me see Keefer until we reached a settlement. We talked several times by telephone; I tried to convince her that she was being unreasonable about Keefer, that for his sake she should allow me to see him for a few hours on the weekends at the house (I thought that was the safest way), but she said I was a confusing son of a bitch and if I had anything more to say about it I should call her lawyer, Clyde Swink. Clyde was the best divorce man in town.

"Try confusing *him*, hotshot!"

Out of a sense of self-preservation (maybe he'd tipped her his plans for me), I asked her if she'd talked to her father. She said he'd called the same week she'd kicked me out. Somehow, he'd gotten the bad news.

"He said, 'Whatchu do? Eh? You throw out your marriage like garbage because some skirt who don't mean nothin'?'

"I said, 'It's over, Daddy.' I told him that we were finished. He got really mad. He said, 'You finished, eh? I *tell* you when you finish! You got some *ragazzo*? Some putzi you like? You think I can't find 'em? I talk to him, eh? I explain to him for you. I give him good counsel. Then you see how fast he run.' Can you imagine him threatening me like that?"

"Linda, you don't have a boyfriend, do you?"

"No, no! Daddy thinks I must be up to something. That's the way his mind works. But we've had it with this charade, right?"

"Yeah, right, I guess; but if you have a boyfriend, he could be in trouble."

"You and my father! Nobody tells me what to do anymore!"

It was a sign her nerves were as jittery as mine. It also made me suspect there might be something to the accusation. I told her she was a grown-up lady. Nobody could tell her what to do. After I got her calmed down, she said Phil threatened to cut her out of his will if she didn't patch it up with me. "I said I didn't need his money. 'Give it all to stupid, if you want.' Daddy's got no power over me anymore. For the first time in a long time I feel like I can breathe, you know? You and I are going to work out a settlement. I'll be fine. I don't need his money. Besides I can always go to Mario after Daddy's gone. Mario won't turn me down, if I need help."

"What about Keefer?"

"What about him?"

"Phil wouldn't--"

"No! Daddy would never do anything to hurt Keefer. He's

safe with me. For all the threats and bluster, he's not going to hurt me, either; but I don't know about you. You better lay low for a while."

"Thanks a lot. That's very reassuring."

"Hey, I'm here to help. That's another reason I'm not letting you near Keefer. If he's with you, Daddy might try to kidnap him. Our marriage has always been about Keefer. You and I were marginal players. I'm keeping him close until this blows over."

"What about school?"

"School, schmool! We'll catch up later."

After this conversation, it seemed to me there was little point in hiding out in hotels. I had the feeling that my every move was being calculated as part of a glide path to the eventual expiation of my sins against the family. But since my fate was out of my hands, I thought I might as well get on with my life--or what was left of it. Immediately, my morning coffee tasted better, and the sun on my face felt so good that I almost cried with gratitude. I rented an apartment and moved in. To be sure, I was careful. I checked under my car for bombs, and every morning before I stepped out the door, I scanned the parking lot for goons. I checked for letter bombs and black balls in the mail; no dead dog turned up on my doorstep as a warning to go home, or else. Phil was a superstitious man; perhaps he was waiting for a propitious date on the calendar, like the appearance of Mars in Taurus. Yet the weeks went by, and nothing happened.

I hired Lloyd Schwanger, an attorney every bit as greasy as Clyde Swink, and within twenty-four hours, Linda agreed that I could spend a few hours with Keefer at the house, but inside, not in the yard. She was still afraid that Phil might kidnap him. We played catch in the basement. Keefer hadn't been to school or outside for weeks. That fall, after the sale of the house, when the crabgrass began to die, and the sun began to sink lower in the sky, and the days grew short and crisp, she decided it was all right for me to pick up Keefer at nine o'clock every Saturday morning and keep him for the day. The master hearings were over. Our final papers would be coming through any day. Now that everything was settled, I thought she was beginning to relax. She was, but not for the reason I thought. Keefer disabused me of my mistake one morning on the way to the apartment.

"Mom's got a boyfriend."

"She has?"

"Yeah, you should see him. He's about a hundred years younger than she is. He's got a motorcycle and long hair. You should see her on it. Boy, does she look silly."

"What's his name?"

"Wesley."

I began to laugh.

"What's so funny?"

"I don't know. It sounds funny. Your mother with a boyfriend named Wesley."

Funny, like when you hit your funny bone. *Finito*, I thought. It finally hit me that it was over in a way that the sale of the house and the divorce settlement had not. What was left was Saturdays with Keefer. It seemed a hard bargain, but a good one.

This is how it worked. Every Saturday morning, I would pull into the parking lot of Linda's apartment house. I would carefully scan the parking lot for possible kidnapers. Satisfied there were none in sight, I would sound the car's horn: *bap! bap!* The door of the apartment house would fly open, out would tumble Keefer on the dead run, hugging a grocery bag of toys with his scruffy old teddy bear riding on top of the pile. I can see him now running across the lawn toward the car, waving wildly, beaming from ear to ear. It was the highlight of my week when my boy came bursting through the door. He dove into the car full of excitement.

"Where we going today, Dad? We going to see the wolves in Lititz? Are we going down to see the white tigers? Aw, you said we could! Come on, Dad! The Phillies playing at home tonight!"

How could I nurse my worries in the face of this smiling boy? My mug bagged into a smile as he clamored into the car, making life lively again, repeating his Saturday war cry: "Where are we going, Dad? Huh? Huh?"

One weekend in late October, one of Linda's Uncle Tonys and his family came through town on their way to Williamsburg, Virginia. This Uncle Tony was big in bananas in Brooklyn. They had children around Keefer's age, and they wanted to take him along.

"You don't mind giving him up for this one Saturday, do you?"

"Suddenly the Banana King calls, and it's all right for Keefer to go away for the weekend?"

"We don't have to worry about that anymore. I had a talk with Mario. Daddy's over it. He's so sick he couldn't cause trouble, even if he wanted to."

"Thanks for letting me in on it. How long have you known this?"

"Maybe a month. I was going to tell you—"

"So I can stop looking under my car for bombs?"

"Don't give me any melodrama, Earl. Daddy would never hurt you. You know that."

"No, I don't know that."

"Well then, you're stupid. So what do you say? You give up Keefer this Saturday, and we work out a new deal?"

"Does he have to wear a Kevlar vest?"

"Very funny."

For granting this little favor, the new deal was from now on I would get to have him for the entire weekend. It sounded good to me. So off he went in Uncle Tony's big white Lincoln, three little kids happy as larks in the back, and Tony and his wife, Rosie, in the front, grinning like they'd just cornered the banana market.

I had a few martinis that Sunday afternoon and fell asleep on the couch in front of an old William Powell-Myrna Loy flick on TV. It was a slow gray rainy day. When the telephone rang, I threw the papers off and fumbled for the receiver. It was Linda.

"Remember what you said if I ever needed any favors?"

"Sure. What's up?"

"I need you to come to the hospital. I'm still covered by the Blue Cross plan, right?"

"Yes, both you and Keefer."

"Daddy's going to get me my own coverage, but he's been so sick--"

I sat up.

"Linda, what's wrong? Did you hurt yourself?"

"Wesley and I had a little accident on his motorcycle. We hit a tree."

"Jesus, are you okay?"

"Actually they say I broke my leg. I got a bump on my head. Otherwise I'm fine. Wesley's okay too. You're okay, aren't you, Wesley?"

A sleepy voice mumbled in the background. She laughed, but I couldn't make out what the answer was. She put her hand over the receiver and said something else to him. It was one of those rude interludes newly infatuated couples indulge in, in front of other people. I waited for it to be over. She wasn't doing it to make me jealous. Fat chance. Besides, she wasn't like that. She might be thoughtless, she might be rude, but she was perfectly guileless. I thought of Florida and Vinny Palumbo. Then I remembered her little episode with Arthur. I began to wonder if I really had grounds to draw any conclusions about her at all. She finished her parenthetical chat with Wesley and came back to me.

"Wesley's a little out of it right now. He broke a leg too."

"I'll be right over," I said.

"Mind bringing me a pack of cigarettes?"

"Sure. Still smoking Winstons?"

I found them in the emergency ward, propped up like dolls on beds across the aisle from each other. His bed was a little closer to the door, but I didn't notice him right away.

"Wes, say hello to Earl."

I had walked right past him. I looked over my shoulder and smiled hello. A long-haired bearded youth with a bandaged nose and a cast on his leg looked at me out of black glittering eyes. They were as soulfully sad as the blue eyes of Jesus on a prayer card. He managed a feeble wave. It was followed by the limp collapse of his hand onto his chest.

I turned back to her and held out the cigarettes. She tore open the pack and lighted one up and sucked greedily on the noxious thing. She carefully blew the smoke against the wall and away from me, knowing that I hated the poisonous stuff, which was more than she used to do when we were married.

She raised the cigarette to her parted lips. It was a pretty gesture, more than the reason warranted. I saw the bandage on her wrist. Her leg was raised and splinted. Otherwise she looked unharmed. Her color was good. She looked rested and happy. She pushed some ringlets off her forehead with the back of her hand and shook her head to make her thick curly hair fall into place.

"Fractured tibia," she smiled shyly. "Some fool, huh? Riding around on a motorcycle at my age."

"Why not, if you're having a good time."

"You talk to them about the coverage?"

"It's taken care of."

"Thanks. It was nice of you to come right over."

"How's your dad?"

"He's bad. Real bad. I'm worried about him. He's lost so much weight. You wouldn't recognize him. Mario is thinking about putting him back in the hospital. You really ought to call him. He still thinks the world of you."

"I didn't think he wanted to talk to me."

"He was mad at you for a while. But he's over it. Call him. You should go up and see him."

"Maybe I should step into oncoming traffic."

"What a candy ass. Where did you get your balls? Out of gumball machine?"

"Maybe I should hang myself with one of my neckties. Get it over with."

But she didn't hear me. She was gazing into one of the far corners of the room, with that open-mouthed look she got on her face when she was in what passed for deep thought.

"I was going up, to be with him. Now this."

"You're in the clear. You can still go up, can't you?"

"Yeah, you're right. Now that things are patched up, I can get Mario to send Cousin Vito down with the car."

"That's a good idea."

"I can still get up there. No problem. What do you think of Wesley?"

"What do I think? I just met him."

"He looks like a kid, doesn't he?"

"Not that young. The beard helps. How old is he?"

"Twenty-five. I could be his mother."

"Thirty-nine? You look as young as he does."

"You really think so?"

"Absolutely."

"He feels awful. He keeps telling me he's sorry. Isn't that like a kid? Maybe you could cheer him up on your way out."

I saw no reason not to stop by his bed. He really did look miserable. He was lying on his pillows with a thin forearm, like the bare branch of a young sapling, resting above the thrust of his bandaged nose. He was suffering tragically in the fashion of young people everywhere.

"How are you feeling?"

Startled, he withdrew his arm and blinked his uncanny bright eyes. He was going to have a nice pair of shiners in the morning. He seemed stunned that I would speak to him. For some reason I shook his hand, which added to his confusion, but afterwards he didn't seem to want to let go. I stood there holding his hand while he told me how bad he felt.

"Are you in a lot of pain?"

"No, no. I feel awful about *her.*"

His face contorted and he looked away. He stretched his jaws as if trying to relieve a pressure bubble in his ear. He touched his heavily taped nose. I wasn't sure what was going on, until I saw a heavy tear slide down his cheek and disappear into his beard. He swiveled his head on the pillows and looked at me earnestly.

"She's such a wonderful person. I took her out on that bike and ran her into a tree. I never even tipped it over in three years. Then I take her out and do this. I might have killed her."

"Don't be so hard on yourself. She's all right."

"I can't believe it. I take her out and nearly kill her. It's like my whole life is cursed."

"Think of it as lucky. You could be a lot worse off."

"If anything happened to her I'd kill myself."

His eyes turned blind. He squeezed my hand and turned his face to the wall again. He was certainly an emotional fellow. I wondered what he did for a living. I thought she'd told me he was a schoolteacher. An art teacher, wasn't that it?

"She's the greatest woman I ever met. This sounds bad, but I'm glad she kicked you out. Little Keith is great too. I'm really crazy about them. Now I guess I've ruined everything."

"Not at all. She thinks you're great too."

"She does? You mean she's not mad at me?"

"Naw. This is nothing. Besides, how many people can say they ran into a tree together on a motorcycle? It's a story you'll be laughing about and telling people the rest of your lives."

"Oh, I don't know," he said darkly. "I don't think it's that simple."

"Are they keeping you overnight?"

"I think so. Why?"

"Get them to give you something to knock you out. Believe me, everything will look better in the morning."

"I will, thanks."

So much for emergencies, I thought, and laughed at the idea of counseling my replacement. It was a story I thought I'd be telling for laughs, too, if I lived long enough. I was giggling to myself about this when I unlocked the door to my apartment the next day after work and stepped inside. It was six o'clock, well after dark. I heard a voice intone from the darkened living room, "You know nothing."

I hit the floor.

"What are you doing on the floor?" the voice said.

"I got a bad knee. Sometimes it goes out from under me, like now. How are you, Vinny?" I said as I got up. "What are doing in my apartment?"

There was Vinny Palumbo, the rumble of his deep voice easily recognizable, sitting in the dark in a chair by the couch. He'd drawn the draperies over the sliding doors that led onto my balcony overlooking the apartment house swimming pool. Now he snapped on the light on the little table beside his chair and gestured for me to take a seat on the couch.

"How did you get in my apartment?"

"A six-year old could get in your apartment. You should get a bolt-action lock. These apartments would be so easy to rob. Some night, you could walk in on a thief. Then what?"

We sat there, looking at each other, thinking that one over.

"Tell no one about this visit. It never happened."

"Right. How have you been?"

"Please. You're such a jerk. I got a couple things to say, then I'm outa here. I'm under strict orders not to see you on this trip. Your father-in-law—your former father-in-law—would be unhappy if he knew. But I thought I should tell you."

He was dressed in a good chalk-striped gray suit with a diamond patterned red tie held in place by a tie clip over his bulging stomach. He was one of those men who when seated have to sit with their legs apart to make room for their bellies and genitals. He had on highly polished, expensive wing-tipped gunboats at least size thirteen the color of cognac. He had a big heavy face that reminded me of the jurist, Antonin Scallia. His receding hair line was plastered against his skull with some goop probably out of one of Phil's barbershops. He looked very professional, every bit a man burdened with serious responsibilities. He paused, his dark eyes under his heavy eyebrows studying me sadly.

"I had the unpleasant task of coming to this shit hole you call a town to tell Linda that her father has written her out of his will."

"I think she was expecting that."

"Nevertheless, she took it badly."

"When did you see her?"

"I just came from her apartment."

"Did you use a credit card?"

"You're a tremendous wise-ass, aren't you?"

"Yes, I've been told that."

"Do you know that she has someone new in her life? Do you even care?"

"Wesley. No, I don't care. I met him yesterday at the Pressman Clinic. They had a little accident on his motorcycle."

"What's your impression of this boy? Do you think he is good for her?"

"I guess he's all right. How would I know?"

"What do you think her father should do about this?"

"Do?"

"Yes. I think your former father-in-law would be influenced by your opinion, if I could find a discreet way of conveying it to him. He would take what you have to say very seriously."

"I have nothing bad to say about this man. I have no advice for Phil. Not now, not ever."

"You know what I think?" Vinny leaned closer to me. I said nothing. I didn't want to know what he thought. But he told me anyway.

"I think," he said. "I think if she really likes this guy, they should run."

CHAPTER | SEVEN

They took their cue from Vinny and ran, taking my son with them. For weeks I had no idea where they were, or whether they were safe. I had no choice but to call the only people that might know where they were. I called Vinny's office first, but Gladys, his long-time secretary, told me Mr. Palumbo was "unavailable." After some hesitation, she told me that she hadn't heard from him in a week.

Reluctantly, not knowing what kind of a reception I'd get, I dialed the Gagliano compound. I figured either Mario or Cousin Vito would answer. Phil didn't answer phones as a rule; besides I'd been told repeatedly that he was sick, which made it even less likely. Linda was close to her brother; if anybody knew anything, it would be him—that is, if he would agree to talk to me. As I expected, Mario picked up. The first thing he said was, "Maybe you shouldn't be callin' here."

"I know, Mario, but I'm desperate. Do you know where Linda is?"

"She ain't here."

"Do you know where she is?"

"She don't tell me nuthin.'"

"So she's called you?"

"I shouldn't be talkin' to you. You did a bad thing."

"I know, I'm sorry. How's your father?"

"He's bad, Early. Real bad."

"I'd like to come up and see him. You think that would be all right?"

"I guess so. I dunno. Maybe I better ask. He was pretty mad at you, y' know."

"Mario, Linda and her boyfriend ran off. They took Keefer with them. I want to know if he's okay."

"Yeah, he's okay. You got nuthin' to worry about. Linda's a good mother."

"I'm his father. Where are they?"

"I'm tellin' you I don't know. She was afraid if I knew, I'd tell Pop. I probably would, too. I don't think what she's doing is right."

"What's going on? Come on, Mario. Be fair."

"Like I say, I don't know."

"I'm coming up there, Mario. I'll bring the cops if I have to. I've got a right to be with my son."

"Who's stopping you? Bring the army."

"Let me talk to Phil."

"He can't come to the phone. He's too sick."

"Come on, Mario. Be a pal."

"He couldn't talk to you anyway. They took out his voice box two weeks ago."

"His voice box? Jesus, what's going on?"

"He's got throat cancer. Didn't Linda tell you? They don't think he's got a chance. But they said he oughta have it out, so I said okay. You know what got him? Not the cancer. He couldah fought it off with a coupla cigars. You and Linda breakin' up, that's what got him."

"Ask if I can see him. Let me know as soon as possible, will you please?"

"He can't talk, but he writes stuff on a pad. I'll ask him and let you know."

"You really can't tell me anything about Linda and Keefer?"

"They was goin' to California. That's all I know. She said they'd be in touch when they got settled."

"Wait a minute! What's this about California? What are you talking about?"

"She tole me they're going to get married and live out there. They're makin' a fresh start out West."

"This comes as an awful shock. I didn't know about any of this."

"Seems like a big change, don't it? Movin' West and all? Especially with Pop being so sick. But you know Linda. Once she makes up her mind–"

"What about me? I'm supposed to have Keefer on weekends. I don't even know where they are."

"She said she'd give you a call once they got settled."

"But she took Keefer with her."

"You didn't expect her to leave him behind, did you?"

"I can't believe this is happening to me."

"Believe it," he said and hung up.

Ten days later, among the bills and circulars in my mailbox, I found a card postmarked San Francisco, with a picture of the Mark Hopkins on it. On the back, it read:

Keefer wants to talk to you. We'll call at 8 P.M. on Sunday night, the fifth. You'd better be home if you want to talk to him.

Linda

It arrived on Tuesday, the seventh. At midnight on the fifth I had been in a taxicab, coming in from the airport after a trip to Columbus, Ohio. I felt like cutting my throat. A week later another card came.

You weren't there, you bum. He was heartbroken. It was a good lesson for him to learn about you. We'll try again at 8 P.M. on the 18th. If you're not there this time, forget it.

Luckily it arrived a few days in advance. I rescheduled a trip to Boston and sat by the phone waiting for the call. Eight o'clock came and went. When it hit quarter after eight, I decided she was operating on Pacific Time. That meant I had nearly four hours to go. I made myself a martini, picked up one of Peter Drucker's books, and settled in for a long read. Maybe I'd take an hour's nap around ten. I wanted to be fresh when I talked to him. The nap would take care of the martinis. Then a little splash of gin in the bottom of a glass would set me up and I'd be ready for the call.

Time passed slowly. I couldn't concentrate on Drucker. He was too much water to carry after a couple of martinis. I put him aside and turned on the television. Somehow the time passed. At ten, I turned off the set and got the clock down out of my shaving kit. I set it for eleven and lay down on the couch for a little nap. I lay there for what seemed a long time, the clock ticking like a little time bomb.

I woke groggy and irritable about eleven-thirty and staggered to the bathroom and splashed some cold water on my face. I didn't look very good in the mirror. You drink too much, I told myself. I went into the kitchen and poured myself a beer. At five of twelve, the telephone rang.

"Person-to-person call for Mr. Earl Bogwell."

"This is Mr. Bogwell."

"I have a person-to-person call for you from Linda Malloy."

My voice was actually trembling.

"So it's Linda Malloy now. You didn't waste any time, did you?"

"Fuck off, wiseguy. You want to talk to him or not?"

"No offense. I just wondered what the hurry was."

"What I do is my business! I don't have to explain myself to you! You got that straight?"

"Right. I've got that straight."

"Okay. Now he's been bugging me to call you. I don't think it's such a hot idea, but he's been driving me crazy about it. He's got his own ideas, I'll give him that. So, okay. Here's the deal. You don't ask him where he's calling from, where's he's staying, or anything like that. You respect our privacy, understand? I'll be on the extension, so no tricks. Get it?"

"Linda-"

"That's the deal. Take it or leave it."

"I'll take it."

"Okay. You've got two minutes."

"I haven't talked to him for a month."

"Two minutes. Take it or leave it."

"Okay, okay."

"Remember, wiseguy. I'll be listening."

The next words I heard were, "Hello, Dad?"

It cut through me like a spear. I was surprised how much it hurt.

"Hello, son. Boy, it's good to hear your voice again. How are you?"

"I'm fine, Daddy. How are you?"

"I'm swell, baby. You sound so grown-up. I really miss you."

"I miss you too, Daddy. When can I come home?"

"I don't know. Your mother and I will have to talk about it."

"Can't you come and get me? I wanna come home. I don't like it out here."

"Hey," Linda said.

"Baby, I would come and get you in a second-"

"Hey!"

"-but I don't know where you are."

"Okay, wiseguy! You blew it. Hang up, Keefer."

"Daddy!"

"Write to me, Keefer! Call me again, baby!"

"Dad!"

"Give me that phone."

I heard him yell, "I wanna talk to him! I wanna talk to my dad!"

The phone went bonk-bonk in my ear. He was bawling angrily.

"Lemme talk to him! I wanna talk to him!"

A chair dragged across the floor, followed by the thump of something heavy. "You little brat," Linda said.

In the background, a man's voice began to murmur: Wesley, the peacemaker.

"I warned you!" I heard Linda yell, followed by more bawling.

I shouted into the phone, "Keefer! I love you, son!"

Their voices trailed off, like she was forcing him down a hall-way into a room at the back of the place, the hotel, the apartment, wherever they were hiding out. Wesley's voice still murmured, counseling restraint. Somebody picked up the phone.

"Still there, Earl?"

"Wesley? Is that you?"

"Yes, hi. Sorry about the uproar. How are you?"

"Pretty lousy, frankly. Where are you people?"

"Here's Linda. She can explain it better than I can."

"Earl?"

"Linda, what the hell-"

"Shut up and let me talk. Okay?"

"Okay. But make it good."

"Vinny Palumbo came by the apartment out of the blue and said I should take off. He said he'd go with me. He said Wesley was 'a problem,' and I should dump him for his own safety. Can you believe that? Making me a proposition like that? I always liked Vinny—but not that much! Anyway I was scared, so we took off."

"When do I find out where you are?"

"Maybe after Christmas."

"Christmas! That's another six weeks."

"We gotta have some space. Keefer's having trouble accepting the situation. Wesley plans to spend a lot of quality time with him."

"No wonder. You practically kidnapped him."

"Hey, watch your language, wiseguy! I don't like that kind of talk."

"Okay, okay. Don't hang up on me. When are you going to call again?"

"I said Christmas, didn't I?"

"How about Thanksgiving?"

"Too soon."

"Give me a break, Linda."

"I'll talk it over with Wesley. We'll let you know."

On that conciliatory note, we ended our call. They rang again at Thanksgiving. This time we were both careful and the conversation went along smoothly. She said I could write to Keefer if I liked. Swink would see that the letters were forwarded. Aha! Swink, Keeper of Secrets! Short of torture, I knew he'd never tell me where they were. I wrote, but I didn't hear from Keefer in reply, except for one three-line, cautiously worded note on tablet paper. He said he was having a good time and liked the weather out there. It was like being at Grampy's down in Florida.

My way of fighting fear and depression has always been to dive into the mind-dimming nature of my work for Frankenwood and Son. So let's dig some up, I thought. I called Atley Turner, the exec at the Society of Texas Hardware and Recycling Dealers. Atley was an influential member of the national board. He and I had become friendly over the years; I thought he might tell me what the board thought of the presentation I'd made in Atlantic City. Months had passed and I hadn't heard a word. What he had to say made my blood run cold.

"I'm in no shape to talk, Earl. We're in turmoil here. One of our staff has gone missing. Nobody's seen her for over a week. Yingluck Honniger? Maybe you remember her from Atlantic City."

He told me the cops found her car in one of the long-term parking garages at Bush International, her purse and keys on the front seat. No evidence that she'd got on any flight. Her husband, Rodney, went on TV and pleaded for her to come home.

"I know whatever is wrong between us, we can fix it," he said and then broke down and had to be led off camera.

The police were unimpressed. They turned up evidence that the couple had been having marital problems. The cops had been summoned to the house on two occasions. They named him "a person of interest."

"I hate to say it," Atley said, "but it looks like Rodney may have hurt her."

In the end, Honniger was charged with murdering his wife. In court it came out that she had been having an affair with Atley. It amounted to quite the bomb shell and resulted in a hung jury.

The District Attorney decided not to try the case again. He didn't have to; public opinion did his job for him. Atley lost his position at the dealers' association and his wife divorced him. Shortly afterwards, one night under a full moon, he drove out into the desert and put a bullet in his brain. Rodney, the aggrieved husband, moved to Arizona to get away from the vicious rumors circulating around town. People in Houston remain convinced that he got away with murder.

Some months later, a female torso washed up on a beach on North Padre Island, 230 miles south of Houston. Volunteers cleaning the beach after a violent storm found it tangled in the brown seaweed that sometimes comes ashore all the way from the Sargasso Sea, hard as that is to believe. DNA testing led authorities to conclude the woman was probably of Asian descent, but the body (if you can call it a body) was so badly decomposed there was no way to make a positive ID. At first they speculated it might be Yingluck, but then decided as likely the woman had been killed, dismembered, and tossed overboard by smugglers engaged in human trafficking. The case was never solved.

When I told Linda about it, she said, "I guess that's what you get when you fuck around with other people's husbands. God catches up with you when you do shit like that."

I couldn't help myself.

"You didn't tell your father to make her go away, did you?"

"What? Some *putain* you bopped disappears, and you want to blame me for it? You sick twisted bastard! Get off my line!"

CHAPTER | EIGHT

It was dark and cold the morning I stepped out of the apartment building and started for Bergen Cove to see Phil. I had called Mario again to see if it was okay; he said if I was coming, I had better hurry because Phil was in bad shape. The darkness made me shiver. It was charged like a sponge with the impenetrable black ink of cold winter mornings. The first light was not encouraging either, with the sky the color of pond ice. But by the time I reached the Berks County line, it had warmed into a brilliantly blue enamel lending a special texture like impasto brushwork to the corn stubble in the farmers' fields. I pulled off my jacket. I turned the heater off. It became one of those soft warm days full of shadow and sunlight that sometimes fall to hand like ripened fruit at the end of autumn.

When I got to the house Cousin Vito was out in the driveway under the trees, looking like Lon Chaney in makeup for his role in *Phantom of the Opera.* He was polishing Phil's big car. He smiled a ghastly smile in greeting.

"Gettin' it ready in case he wants ta go for a ride," gesturing at the car with the polishing rag in his bony hand. He lifted the chauffeur's cap he wore cocked over a large pendulous ear and scratched his head with the bill. He was at least as old as Phil, but there wasn't a gray hair among the sparse black threads on his head. He shrugged his shoulders.

"What can it hurt, right?"

Mario was coming down the steps from the house as Cousin Vito said this.

"How many times I gotta tell ya? He's not goin' for any rides! He's dyin', for Chrissakes! When you gonna wake up?"

"Well, we could ask. Maybe some fresh air, maybe if I drove him out to Montauk Point--"

"Awww, why do I waste my time talkin' to you!"

Mario made a violent dismissive gesture, not unlike Phil in the old days. He took my elbow and guided me toward the house.

"That dumb goombah. He still thinks Pop's gonna make it."

Mario told me to ready myself. He said Phil looked awful. He had lost some more weight during his latest stay in the hospital, and was now down to a hundred pounds.

"When they dressed him at the hospital, the dumbos forgot to put his underwear on. So I lift him out of the backseat and lean him against the car, ya know, so I can reach in for the suitcase. And his goddam pants fall down. He's standing there in his shirt-tails. I figure I'm really gonna get one for this!"

Mario said he was perfectly positioned for a drop kick to the tail section. He shut his eyes and braced himself. When nothing happened, he opened his eyes and backed out of the car. He thought maybe Phil was waiting for him to turn around so he could give him a few bracing slaps across the face. But then he realized Phil was standing there, hogtied by his own trousers. With one vague hand, he was touching the handkerchief at his throat. With the other, he was holding onto the car so he wouldn't fall down along with his pants. He was looking around in bewilderment, as if uncertain where all the fresh air was coming from.

Mario said he never wanted a kick in the pants or a slap across his face so bad in his life. It made him feel like bawling to see his father standing there looking around meekly with his pants on the ground. Cousin Vito was still sitting in the car, having taken this moment to re-comb his hair in the rearview mirror. He combed it forward. He combed it straight back. Then he parted it and combed it to either side. Mario stood there and watched him in amazement.

"Gimme some help, you moron!"

He pulled up his father's trousers and told him to hold on to them. He held him under the arms and Cousin Vito grabbed his feet. Together they carried him up the steps and into the house, where Anna helped them put him to bed. He had remained there ever since.

"He's never gettin' out of bed again. It's hard, but I gotta accept it. For him, it's the end. Stupid, out there polishing the car, telling me I ought ask if he wants to take a ride out to Montauk Point. He's got rocks in his head. We got nurses for him twenty-four hours a day. What's he think? He's gonna come out on the steps someday and say, 'Yoohoo, Cousin Vito! I grew a voice box overnight, 'n' I wanna go for a ride.' That dumb goombah! They oughta lock 'em on a farm somewhere."

For the first few days, Mario told me, Phil seemed to make a rapid recovery. He started acting like his old self again. He sat up in bed. He pushed the nurse away when she tried to change the handkerchief and clean his whistle gadget. He wrote incessant messages with the pencil and paper kept at the ready on the nightstand by his bed. FOOD, he scrawled in big letters, trying to make the paper bark with his old voice of authority. DRINK, he demanded. TV, he wrote when he wanted entertainment. Sometimes he would scribble FUCK OF; by which Mario understood his father wanted to be left alone. Mario would take the pretty young nurse by the elbow and leave the old man to himself for a few minutes.

"He don't spell so hot, but he gets the message across."

Gradually the onslaught of his furiously scribbled messages began to subside. He had no particular fluency when it came to words on paper. He had always depended on voice inflection and gesture to give his orders the proper shading. He scribbled and slashed at the page. He tried to supplement with grimaces and furious nods and shakes of his head. When Mario or the cute little nurse misunderstood what he wanted and brought him the wrong thing, he threw whatever it was on the floor. The bigger the mess, the louder the crash, the better he liked it. It was as close as he ever came to having a voice again.

Slowly, however, his tantrums gave way to sullen indifference, loss of appetite, and long snoring naps. This was the state he was in now. Except for a few hours each day, when he roused himself to glare like a wounded hawk at the friends and relatives who timidly streamed through his room every afternoon between the hours of three and four to pay their respects.

As I passed the dining room I noticed a painting over the sideboard that looked like a good copy of Vermeer's "The Concert," one of the paintings taken in the Gardner Museum heist in 1978. Thirteen pieces had been stolen, valued at an estimated five hundred million dollars. None had ever been recovered. Evidently late in life, Phil had become an art lover. The man was full of surprises.

My special midmorning audience didn't last long. Mario had rented a hospital bed. The head of it was cranked up partway and the railings raised. The bosomy young nurse had propped him up on his pillows for the occasion. He lay on the high hard shelf of his bed with his pad and pencil in his lap, his bony knees draped in the sheeting wound around his legs. Secure behind his railings, he looked like some awful scrawny wizened baby or a recently hatched out California condor. His glittery eyes darted in my direction for a second when I entered the room, blinked as if shocked at the sight, then fixed stubbornly on the drawn draperies of the windows opposite his bed, which, if open, would have given him a view of his fallow garden and grape arbor. I thought this would be his revenge for my desertion: that he would not look at me from his deathbed. But no. That was apparently not it. He needed to look away in order to collect himself. He could do that more easily by avoiding my eye. Mario indicated a chair a few feet from the bed. I sat down and waited. Mario stood by my chair to act as interpreter.

Phil attempted a few messages. He closed his gnarled fingers around the pencil stub. He couldn't hold it very well. He kept dropping it into the chasm of his lap. The young nurse kept retrieving for him. She giggled the third time it happened.

"You just like me to tickle you."

He stabbed at the writing tablet impatiently, hopelessly, trying to make it speak for him. The dots and slashes on the paper looked totally unintelligible to me, as they passed from the nurse's hand, over my head, to Mario. But he made sense out of them somehow.

"He sez: You don't look so hot."

"Probably not, Phil. I've been working hard."

More frantic stabbing with the pencil, until the point snapped off.

The nurse giggled again.

"You're a little devil today, aren't you?"

She pushed back the chair at her little desk by his bed, came around the front. With a tinkly laugh, she fumbled the pencil stub out of his emaciated lap again. She sharpened it at the pencil sharpener screwed to the edge of her miniature desk. When she held it out, he grabbed it from her roughly. He scribbled some more. He tore off the sheet and passed it to the nurse, who passed it over my head to Mario.

"He sez-" Mario looked at me darkly. Big grapey shadows darkened the sockets of his eyes as he struggled with his emotions.

"He sez- he sez he loved you like a son. You were a child given to him by God in his old age. You n' Keeper. Now youse is both dead. He sez: you guys broke his heart."

More scribbling. He paused to give me a sidelong look out of his narrow glittery eyes. It was a look of utter hatred and contempt. He ripped the paper from the pad and thrust it at the nurse, who glanced at it before she passed it over my head to Mario with a flirtatious little smirk. Phil patted the handkerchief at his throat to make sure it was still in place. He raised his hip in the air and heaved himself onto his side, turning his face to the draperied wall. The interview was over. I had been dismissed. I was to leave the house now. Condemned, I assumed, to mull over in perpetuity my sins against the family. There was no need for Mario to translate the final message, but he did anyway.

"He sez-oh yeah," the disk of Mario's dark face brightened. He seemed considerably cheered by the runic scribble on the crumpled scrap of paper he clutched in his hairy fist. He tried to suppress the flicker of a shamefaced smile as he delivered Phil's final volley. I recognized the anguished ambiguity in that twitching grin of his. It was a smile long famigliar to me. It was the smile of a benchwarmer son.

"He sez: You're stupid. You should go away now, so he can die in peace."

"I understand, Phil. I'm sorry we let you down."

I started for the door.

"Wait a minute! Wait a minute! He's tryin' to say somethin' else."

Phil was flailing at the bedcovers, in a terrific tangle of sheets, struggling to turn over and face us again. The nurse rushed forward to help him. I heard a bubbly aspiration of impatience escape his lips. Around the edge of her starched white sleeve, I saw his eyes were on me again. He made a violent gesture. I thought he was giving me the finger.

"He wants you over by the bed."

Phil watched my approach avidly. His skull looked fragile as an eggshell. He kept his shiny eyes on me. He looked severe and unforgiving. He had about him something of the fanatical glitteriness you see in the old photographs of Rasputin. He made another violent gesture, which I didn't understand.

"He wants you to get down on your knees," Mario said, and added in a choked voice, "I think he wants to give you his blessing."

I did as I was told.

He gestured again, for me to come nearer to the bed. I moved a few paces closer on my knees. He grabbed me roughly by the ear and used it to crank me up so he could take a good look at me. His eyes slowly filled with tears. He shook his head and smiled sadly. He made a vague despairing gesture in the air. I supposed it was the sign of his benediction. He took my head in both hands like a bowling ball. I felt his dry lips touch my forehead. Then he pushed me away and faced the wall again.

In the hallway, Mario gave me a doleful look.

"He always liked you better 'n me. Don't it seem a little unfair to you?"

"He loves you, Mario."

"Yeah, I know. I just wished he *liked* me. Ya know what I mean?"

I knew what he meant. Knew it chapter and verse.

Outside on the gravel, he said, "Come back 'n' see us sometime. What happened between you 'n' Linda, that's history. It's got nothin' to do with us, right? So come back 'n' see us. Me and Cousin Vito, we're gonna be lonelier 'n shit when that old crook in there kicks the bucket."

"I will."

Something in my voice caused him to raise his head. Whatever he saw in my face made the light go out of his eyes.

"No. No, you won't."

"Sure I will."

"Naw. You'll never come back. That's the way it is. Right? People have their own lives to live. To hell with everybody else."

"I'll come back. I promise."

"Yeah, sure. Take care of yourself. I always liked you. You're a good guy."

We shook hands and left it at that. I got in my car and circled the drive and drove out through the gates. I never saw him again. A week later, I had a card from him telling me Phil had died.

CHAPTER | NINE

A fter Phil died, Linda felt safe and told me they were living outside of Santa Barbara.

"Who knows? You could drop dead tomorrow. You could have an accident. People get killed all the time."

I thought it was nice of her to remind me.

I visited Keefer in the middle of December. I took him down to Disneyland for the weekend; he'd already been there several times, thanks to Wesley, but he was happy to go back again and give me the guided tour, since it was my firsttime. He was pleased to see me, but not beside himself by any means. Wesley was being exceptionally good to him. He told me Wesley had promised to buy him a motorcycle when he got old enough. Since I wasn't around anymore, he said Wesley was his father now. The cruelty was unintentional, just a matter of fact. They were going to tour up and down the coast, maybe even travel into British Columbia. Wesley told him it was the most beautiful place in the world. Nothing, he said, could match travel by motorcycle.

"I thought he'd had enough of that when he ran your mother into a tree."

Keefer looked shocked at the brutality of my slur against the great and noble pastime of motorcycling.

"He says it's safe if you know what you're doing. It's safer than a car."

Other than that spiteful outburst, I kept my opinions to myself. I admit I was jealous that Wesley had taken my place so quickly. Wesley! Oh, Wesley, you think you're safe because Phil is dead, but if I were you I'd be scared out of the jacket of my skin; I'd be naked afraid, all pulsing veins and arteries, my hair standing up on my head, puffed out like a scared cat's tail. You converse calmly; you act like all this is normal. Where did you get such a foolish idea?

According to the stories, God has legions of angels at His disposal to do His work; He can dragoon the Devil and his minions for special projects. They think they're the independent opposition, but He's got them in His pocket. Then there are the humans, willing fools, who will do anything He puts into their heads. Phil has only humans, but even posthumously you can be sure he will use them adroitly to accomplish his ends. And while God is known in some circles for His forgiveness, I don't think the same applies to Phil. So sleep the sleep of the innocent, Wesley! You have nothing to worry about!

In the weeks leading up to Christmas, those heavily symbolic days that begin again the age-old cycle of rebirth and retribution, leading inevitably to the death of innocence, I visited my clients in New York, Chicago, and Boston. I did not lay hands on them, but I blessed them after my fashion and eased the burden of their wallets. After all, 'twas the season. My shopping list was short. I put a check and a card in the mail for Keefer. Thank God, Nola was planning on spending the holidays with the Wilhides on their farm outside of Charlottesville, Virginia, so I didn't have her to worry about. I did go out and buy a tree, to make the place look a little more festive. I had a time getting it to stay upright in its stand. After several minutes of squatting and fumbling with the crude turning screws that were supposed to dig into the tree's pitchy trunk and hold it steady, I uncramped to look at the results. It was a little crooked, but it was a nice big tree. Nice and full, no raggedy bare spots. It would look fine when I got the red and blue bulbs and garland on it. I considered wrapping some boxes in gift paper and sticking them under the tree to take away the bareness. If I was going to do this, I thought, I might as well do it right.

As I stood considering this, the tree fell over suddenly and jabbed me in the eye. I bent over and clapped my hand over it. I felt something warmly wet on my fingers. Oh Christ, I thought. It's bleeding. It isn't bleeding, is it? Make it not bleeding. Jesus, not my eye. I drew my hand away and squinted at it. It was daubed with blood. Blood all right: bright and plentiful.

I made it downstairs to the parking lot and got in my car. I cocked my head to one side in some fool notion that it might slow the bleeding and drove to the emergency room at the Pressman Clinic. They took one look and sent for Dr. Moffet, the ophthalmologist.

"Take your hand away," he said.

"I can't."

"I can't work on it if you don't take it away."

Reluctantly, I removed my hand.

"Now open it."

"I can't."

"We'll give you something to numb the pain."

Holding my lower eyelid out, he inserted a hypodermic needle very carefully below my eye. At the puncture, I damned nearly fainted. Almost immediately the pain began to subside. He was able to shine his penlight in there and start to work without causing me any real discomfort.

"You damaged it, all right. Scratched the cornea pretty bad. Clipped a little piece of meat out of the white part. Cut your eyelid pretty good too. You had quite a tussle with that tree."

"It was stupid. I don't know how I did it."

"You'll be all right. What we've got to watch out for is infection. Mainly we have to let it heal. I've bathed it. Take these pain pills. You'll be pretty ouchy for a time. Put this ointment in it three times a day. Take the bandage off and lower the bottom lid and squeeze in about that much. Don't touch it with the tip of the applicator. It won't be comfortable. It'll be sensitive to light."

"You think it's going to be all right?"

"Infection is the main thing. Don't go poking anything else

into it."

"I'm really feeling punk."

"I shouldn't wonder," he said.

I was headachy and feverish. I couldn't wait to get home and take a pill. The pain came and went in spasms and seemed to replicate the original trauma. At its worst, I had to pull over onto the shoulder of the road until it let up. Feeling faint and sweaty, I lay across the front seat and held my head, hoping some dumb cop wouldn't come along and ask me what I was doing. When I got home, I went directly to the bedroom, turned on the electric blanket, and got into bed. I shivered until the heat finally penetrated my bones and nudged me into a state of fitful sleep. I stayed there for fourteen hours, waking only from time to time to swallow another pill.

The next morning, I woke with a fiery pain in my good eye. I felt my way to the bathroom. The eye didn't want to open when I tried to study it in the mirror. It smarted and watered as I squinted at the glass just long enough to understand that I had a rash that ran from my hairline across the right side of my forehead, down into my unpatched eye. It trailed off halfway down my left cheek. The path it made was shiny, purpley-red and pimply. It stung as if I'd stuck my face into a patch of nettles. My eye watered copiously as I worked my way down the hall to the telephone by the sofa in the living room.

"Now you've gone and bunged up the other one," said Moffet in disgust. "You better come in and let me look at it."

"I can't. I can't see. There's nobody here to drive me."

"You couldn't crawl over here, could you? Head north when you get to Second Street."

"That's very funny."

"Well, all right, young fella. I'll make an exception in your case. What's your address?"

He didn't keep me waiting long. I sat on the couch with my eye shut while he got the tools of his trade out of his black bag and fussed with the lampshade. I had a tremendous headache.

"Put your head back."

"I got it back."

"Well, put it back some more."

I grew tired of him squinting down his ocular scope and breathing into my face, a man of the medical trade reduced to a bulging eye and one giant nostril.

"Looks like you have a lovely case of the shingles. You're not going to be very comfortable for the next week or so."

"I don't feel very comfortable now."

"Cheer up. It'll get worse. Can somebody help you out?"

Not really, I thought. There was Nola and there was Arthur. Worse and worser; I chose the former, although there was hardly any daylight between them.

"I hate to bother you, Ma."

"Don't be silly. You've neglected me over the years, but I'm not the type to hold a grudge."

"Really, if you'd rather not–"

"Stop being stuffy. Tell me what you need."

She got a prescription filled and did some grocery shopping. She made a stop at the liquor store. I had decided to switch from gin to vodka, thinking it might go easier on the stomach lining. When she got back, she made a great show of lining up the three bottles of vodka on the coffee table in front of the couch where I was resting.

"Here is your booze. I thought you might like to admire it before I put it away. Look how much there is. It ought to keep you plastered for three or four days."

"I get the point, Ma."

"It didn't do your father much good, did it?"

I agreed it had done him nothing but harm.

"My, my. It's so funny, isn't it?"

I couldn't see, but I could imagine the smile pursing her lips and the faraway look in her eyes.

"What's so funny, Ma?"

"I was thinking how when you're young, things like sex and liquor seem so necessary. When you reach my age you realize how stupid it is. I don't think Mother and Daddy ever slept together after I was conceived. They had more important things to think about."

"I'm sure they did, Ma. Same time tomorrow?"

For a week she ferried me to the doctor's office to have my dressing changed. We didn't talk much on our trips to the doctor. I had all I could do to deal with the nausea that gripped me whenever I left my dark apartment. She tried not to rock me around. Every sudden movement hurt my head. I held onto it with both hands and kept my unbandaged eye shut as we swerved in and out of traffic. One of the advantages of keeping the hurtful light out of my eye was that I couldn't see the stop signs and red lights she ran through. From time to time she would say in an outraged tone: "What is that man shouting about?"

Or: "Why is that fool shaking his fist?"

The lot at the doctor's was small and crowded. She pulled into the no-parking zone out front, left the Rambler babbling in various zany registers at the curb, and walked me to the waiting room. Then she went outside and drove the car around the block until I appeared again on the front steps. She would then repeat the maneuver: leave the maddened Rambler jibbering at the curb, come fetch me, lead me to the car and drive me home. Inside, the medical tech who presided over the outer reaches of Moffet's universe could never seem to guide me through the warren of hallways to the cubicle selected for my examination without running me onto a chair or pushing me into the weighing scales.

"Careful there."

The examination followed, a trial worse than being led blind through the maze by a sadist. I supposed I was taking it all like a baby, and said so once. I was expecting sympathy. Moffet flipped up his goggles.

"That's right. I get people in here with real problems. Much worse off than you."

Humbled, I sat there meek and uncomplaining, as the son of a bitch hurt me again. When it came time for the bandages, it was all I could do to keep from whimpering with relief.

On the way over on the third day, she said: "I hope you get over this fast."

She had no aptitude or patience for nursing any more than I did. On the drive home, she confessed her real worry. She was afraid she wouldn't be able to go down to Charlottesville and spend the holidays with the Wilhides.

"If you don't get better soon, I'll have to cancel my plans."

"Don't be silly. You go."

"Are you sure?"

"Positive."

"Promise? I don't want to miss out on the fun, and you certainly don't qualify as fun."

We both laughed at her little joke.

"Christ, you're awful." My heart went out to her as she sat there looking as pleased as if I had paid her a compliment.

On Christmas morning, I lay on the sofa taking comfort in the steady murmur of the television set. As yet it still hurt to watch it. I thought I might have a drink by way of acknowledging the holidays. I got up and switched channels to catch the news. I shuffled about the apartment, squinting no more than I had to out of the eye with shingles. I had just settled back on the sofa when the story came over the TV.

"Doctors at the Pressman Clinic are looking for people who have an infection called shingles, in order to make a serum to save a boy's life. Perfecto Rivera, six years old, of Lebanon, is suffering from a rare case of internal chicken pox. He is listed in critical condition. Only an antigen taken from the blood of someone suffering from shingles at the right stage of infection can provide the life saving help that the Rivera child needs. The hospital has made several public appeals. If you think you can help, please call--"

By God, I thought, maybe I'm the infected shit they're looking for.

"Yes, we're still searching for a donor," said the doctor they put me onto when I dialed the number mentioned on the news. His name was Levis. He sounded tired.

"How fast can you get here?"

"I can't get there. I can't see."

"You can't see?"

"No. I've got shingles in one eye and I jabbed the other with a Christmas tree."

"I'll send somebody. Sit tight."

When I felt my way into his office, he looked at the crusty mess on my face and broke into a smile.

"You're beautiful. Absolutely goddam beautiful."

He rushed me down the hall, where they hooked me up to some transfusion equipment. I was rolling down my sleeve afterwards when Levis poked his head around the curtain.

"Somebody out here wants to see you."

In a minute, a small dark woman in a bandana appeared around the edge of the curtain and beamed at me. She was carrying a brown paper sack.

"Perfecto's pajamas."

"Pardon me?"

She showed me the paper bag. "My son's pajamas."

Pajamas in a paper bag brought back good memories. And *Perfecto*: what a name. I wish I'd thought of it for my boy.

I said, "I hope he gets better soon."

"Thank you. I can't say enough thanks."

Her eyes shone with such heartfelt gratitude that it embarrassed me.

"Well, I hope it will do some good."

I was afraid of queering the kid's luck by sounding too confident.

"Because of you, my Perfecto will live."

"I'm sure the doctors-"

She shook her head impatiently.

"Not doctors. You. You come from God."

"Actually I heard about it on TV," I said, and immediately felt foolish. "Well, anyway, I hope your boy grows up to be president."

She showed me beautiful teeth.

"If so, we will invite you to the White House."

"Not good enough. I'm not settling for less than Secretary of State."

She showed me those beautiful teeth again.

I doubted that God, if He existed, had sunk so low to use someone of my caliber to carry out His plans. Yet it was probably typical of Him, like Phil, never to work out in the open. Anyway, it was a sweet fairy tale, and if I had the audacity to claim to be the inadvertent agent for this fantasy, I could indulge in the following consolation: while I had lost one boy (two, counting the baby) I had saved another. I was not fool enough to think it expiated my sins against the family (that reckoning was yet to come) but it comforted me to think I had not run the risk of blindness for nothing.

CHAPTER | TEN

I was having lunch between flights at JFK, when a man from the past slipped into the chair opposite me at the table.

"How's the cheesesteak here?"

It was Donkey Man, the sad-eyed guy with the big forehead from another restaurant twenty-five years ago. I knew that even in death Phil couldn't let me off for my defection from the family, but I was surprised it was to come in such a public place. Donkey Man, with his sad face and in his good blue suit, seemed like an unlikely candidate for the job. He looked like a bean counter, a guy you kept in the back room, wearing a celluloid green eyeshade, working out sums on an abacus. Which, on second thought, made him the perfect choice. All this went through my mind before he even extended his hand.

"Mr. Bogwell, I'm Jack Mooney. I don't think we've met," he smiled, which made him look no less sad. "I'm your father-in-law's attorney--your former father-in-law, I should say. Actually, now, attorney for the estate."

"I thought Vinny Palumbo--"

"Yes, well, there was a change recently. I handle things now."

When he reached in his pocket, I flinched. I may have even closed my eyes. He stopped, his elbow in the air, and gave me a sad, reproving look, before holding up a small glittering object between his thumb and forefinger.

"Open," he nodded at my hand clutching the edge of the table and dropped it into my sweaty palm.

"Sorry. I didn't have time to wrap it."

It was a pavé silver tie clip with a line of tiny black diamond chips running horizontally through its center.

"Not exactly The Table of Islam, is it? But it's probably worth a few dollars. It's a gift from Mr. Gagliano. Not Mario—the real one."

He was leaning his elbows on the table and speaking in an affable conversational tone as if we were old friends. I stared at the shiny thing in my hand. I didn't use tie clips. I found them fussy and basically useless. Had Phil overlooked that detail about me? I doubted it. He was pretty sharp. I blew out an explosion of air I'd been holding in ever since Donkey Man had reached in his pocket.

"I don't understand."

"Do any of us really *understand*, Mr. Bogwell? I don't mean to ruin your lunch by being philosophical, but sometimes we should accept things gracefully without trying to parse their deeper meaning. Don't you agree? Anyway, Mr. Gagliano wanted you to have it. I suppose he had his reasons. I can assure you he paid more for it than it is worth. Call it a parting gift."

I sat there dumbly, waiting for him to pull out a gun and shoot me between the eyes.

"Well, I have a plane to catch," he said affably, "and so do you. It's nice to meet you at last, Mr. Bogwell. I've heard about you for years. I doubt if we'll meet again. Ships passing in the night, and so on," he smiled and shook my hand and was gone, leaving me to wonder what the hell had just happened. But he was right; I had a plane to catch. They were already loading at the gate. I put the tie clip in my pocket. When I got home from my trip to Birmingham, Alabama, where I'd given my pitch to a new potential client, I tossed it in a drawer and forgot about it.

Two weeks later I was in Miami and happened to read a follow-up piece in the local newspaper about a suicide a few miles up the coast in a marina in Hollywood. The man had hanged himself aboard a boat he'd kept there for his winter vacations. According to the paper, he'd strung himself up by several neckties wrapped into a ligature. His name was Vincenzo Aurelio Palumbo. It took me a minute to realize what I was reading. Vincenzo: Vinny--Vinny Palumbo had hanged himself!

When I got home I opened the drawer and dug through the shoe box where I kept what I called my jewelry–an onyx ring I'd inherited from Ray, a pair of gold cuff links in the shape of serpents that Linda had given me years ago (her prophetically-inspired final opinion of me)– and found the tie clip with the black diamonds. Engraved on the back of the clip, so tiny I could barely see them, were the letters, *V. A. P.* My legs went out from under me, sending me crashing to the floor. I crawled over to the tie clip and looked again. Yes, I was sure: *V.A.P*: Vinny's initials, the "A" standing for "Aurelio," because I'd told Linda many times that his initials stopped just short of spelling "vapid." No dead dog had been delivered to my doorstep. Donkey Man and the "gift" of the tie clip was a far more subtle approach than a black ball in the mail, or a dead dog on the door mat. Phil had balanced the books on his way out. Our sins, Linda's and mine, had cancelled out each other. Linda lived far away, in the land of fruit and nuts. I doubt anyone ever told her about her former lover's "suicide"—not Mario, not Donkey Man; certainly not me. Truly now, it was *finito*.

III

CHAPTER | ONE

Keefer came East to stay with me when he was fourteen, and I could see he was deeply changed from the happy little boy I remembered. He had long Christ-like hair down to his shoulders and was into heavy metal. It had been a year since I'd seen him. He was now no longer a boy, and not yet a man, that in-between territory where confusion often leads to obnoxiousness.

The visit was not a success. We went up to New York for a weekend and I took him to see some shows, but it bored him silly. There were no children allowed in the apartment complex where I lived, except as short-term guests, so he had no other teenagers to hang out with. At night, he stayed in his room and listened to his Metallica tapes. One morning I found a roach clip under his mattress when I was cleaning his room. I asked him if he was smoking pot. This made him angry, although he didn't answer the question.

"I don't want you smoking dope in this house. You could burn the place down."

He wouldn't talk to me for the rest of the day.

One night, after I went to bed, he got up and took the keys to my car and drove to one of the malls where the local kids hang out, and backed my car into a light pole in the parking lot. When I went out in the morning, I found the rear deck and right fender pushed in. When I asked him if he'd taken the car, he denied it. I don't know why I was so ready to suspect him, rather than concede that somebody must have run into it in the parking lot, as he suggested. When he saw I wasn't going to buy into the anonymous hit-and-run theory, he knitted his dark brows and looked at me thoughtfully.

"You never believe anything I say. You automatically think everything wrong around here is my fault. I really fuck up your little routine, don't I?"

"Watch it, young man. I don't go for that kind of talk."

"Sorry. I mean, I *interfere* with your program of Mozart and martinis. You don't get enough reading time. Your tennis game suffers when I'm around, right?"

"Hey, I'm sorry you find me such a stuffed shirt. I'm not used to having someone else bumping around in the apartment with me."

"I'm your kid. I'm not 'someone else.'"

True. He was my kid, even though he'd told me he wasn't last time the subject came up. I still see the way he looked that morning. I see his long hair, the sparse stubble on his chin, the frowning dark eyebrows; the sudden clearing of perplexity on his young face as he looked away and muttered:

"You don't give a rat's ass about me. I can't wait to get out of here."

"That can be arranged," I said. "How about I call your uncle? I'm sure he won't mind if you turn up a few days early."

"Yeah, right."

"I could call him. Is that what you want?"

"Yeah, that's what I want. At least around him I can be myself."

Good riddance, I thought.

I called Mario to let him know his nephew was on the way. The next day I put Keefer on the *Broadway Limited* for New York. We had our breakfast, we drove to the station, and we waited for the train in utter silence. I had tried to start a conversation with him a few times early that morning. But when he refused to answer, I gave it up. When it was time for him to get on the train, he did not say goodbye. He picked up his duffel bag and slung his guitar over his shoulder by the strap and walked down the stairs to the platform without a word. I did not follow him. Nor did he look up before he got on the train to see if I was still there at the top of the stairs watching him. I left the station feeling very angry.

Linda and I gradually got to the point where we could talk civilly on the telephone. That made it possible for her to tell me about Keefer's troubles, but not until several years later. About a year after his visit with me he was involved in a shooting accident at the house. Wesley had bought him a rifle and was taking him regularly to a nearby shooting range and promised to take him Elk hunting in Montana in the fall, if he got off to a good start in school. It was part of a plan to get him away from a set of bad friends he'd taken up with in the neighborhood; kids from good families, but spoiled with too much time and money on their hands. Linda suspected this was where Keefer had picked up his pot smoking and the backtalk habit.

"The year before, his grades really stunk," she said. "We decided what he needed was some fresh incentives. He was so bored by school."

Wesley had just pulled into the driveway and heard the gun go off. Through the open window in Keefer's room, he heard a boy cry out, "Oh my God, Keefer! Why did you shoot him?"

He rushed upstairs and found some boys in Keefer's room crowded around another boy he'd never seen before. The boy was on the floor, propped up against a bookcase, a bewildered look on his smashed face, bleeding profusely.

Wesley asked them where Keefer was.

He's calling 911, they said.

He asked one of them to get him a towel and he folded it into a pad to staunch the flow of blood from the boy's face. The boy was very brave. He couldn't swallow. His jaw was shattered and his throat kept filling up. He asked Wesley to prop him up higher. He was afraid of choking to death. Wesley held the boy in his arms until the ambulance came.

"Where's Keefer?" he asked the other boys.

"He's in the hall," they said. "He won't come in."

Wesley rode in the ambulance to the hospital with the boy. He stayed in the waiting room while they took him into surgery. The boy's family had assembled by that time. The grandfather gave him hell all the time they waited for not keeping the gun locked up. The boy had three operations over a period of several months, but he survived. If the bullet had hit him square by another half inch it would have killed him. There was a lawsuit, of course, and a big settlement by the insurance company.

"Keefer took it hard. You know how cruel kids can be. When he went back to school, they wanted to know if he'd killed anybody lately. He told me if Kip didn't make it, he'd kill himself. Of course, there was no question of that. The boy was out of danger after the first operation. He wanted me to scrub the bloodstains out of the carpet in his room right away. I scrubbed it with everything I could think of, and got most of it out.

"But he said it kept coming back. He would take me up to his room and show me. You could maybe see a faint outline of something if you looked real hard. I scrubbed it some more, but I couldn't satisfy him. We had a new carpet put in, but he didn't like the room anymore, so we did the guest room over and moved him in there. It was a tough time for him."

The following year, he dislocated his hip in a motorcycle accident. As promised, Wesley had gotten him a two-stroke for his sixteenth birthday. He had it about two weeks and smashed himself and the motorcycle all to hell in one of the canyons near their house in what he called a hill climb in competition with some other kids. The surgeon was concerned the blood supply might have been cut off to the femoral head. He said the bone might begin to die. Keefer went back every six months for regular checkups. Linda asked the doctor how long it would take to know if the bone was all right.

"You know what that jerk told me? He said it was hard to know. He'd seen cases where it didn't go bad for seven years. Seven years! That was reassuring, wasn't it? He said it right in front of Keefer, too. I could have strangled him."

She said he was afraid the hip would go bad and leave him with only one leg. She did her best to assure him that it was unlikely. Still, she worried about it, too, and she said ruefully, "It probably showed."

Not long afterward, the girl he'd been seeing broke up with him. They were "too young to get serious," was the way she put it. Besides he was laid up at home and there was still a month of summer to go. The deprivation was too much for her to bear.

"She picked a bad time for it," Linda said. "His self-esteem was shot, as it was."

Then said, "'Shot.' That's a good one, isn't it?"

It was a sad, sad litany. It threw into relief my lousy behavior like nothing had before. I had not written or called. Holding out. Holding back. As if he owed me an apology from that time he got on the train and left without a word of goodbye. Afraid of giving any sign of love out of my little fund, without the assurance of getting back equal value. It made me sick to think I'd acted like that.

"I don't know," she said. "It was one thing after another with him. I'll never understand it."

When they discovered he was still smoking pot and decided to put him in a detox program, he stopped talking to them. The program was supposed to be for ten weeks; it was operated out of a beautiful estate on the Monterey Peninsula.

"He busted out of there in three weeks. He didn't come home. He went to Los Angeles and lived on the streets for three months before the cops found him and brought him home. You can't imagine how hopeless I felt. I had no idea what to do with him after that."

When I asked her why they hadn't called me when his troubles began to multiply, she said, "I was ashamed. Besides, you had your own life to live."

Said even more gently than Nola, that time in the cemetery when we buried Richie, but it fell on me like a tree.

The day after the Twin Towers collapsed, he joined the army

and was selected for Special Forces training. Soon afterwards, he was deployed to Afghanistan. I saw some of them on TV in native garb and on horseback riding with the Northern Alliance and wondered whether Keefer was one of them. I was sure he was going to be killed out there, but he survived three deployments and came home a changed man. He found meaning in Afghanistan and then lost it again in the total confusion that followed. Otherwise, he might have stayed in and made a career of it.

A lot of boys come home from our thankless wars with PTS, but war cleared Keefer's head as nothing else had. After he completed his service, he came East (he did not visit me; why would he?) and got a job as an apprentice in a boat yard in Rhode Island. The yard built wooden boats in the tried and true old way, held together with treenails ("trunnels," to you and me) and solidly constructed on oak keels. When he had mastered the trade, he built a schooner that he named the "Cherokee," which I thought was ironic; either that, or the result of some remnant memory embedded in his genes, since it was also the name of the ship that his twice removed great-grandfather on Nola's side had captained during the Civil War and in which he had captured two Confederate blockade runners, the *Circassian* and the *Emma Henly*, the two largest prizes ever taken by the U. S. Navy. It is amazing how history follows us around and makes us do stuff we do not understand.

He plied the schooner between Camden Harbor and Key West for three years with a crew of two and took people out for cruises in both locations, then sold the boat and went to work at Mystic Seaport, where he teaches boat building and is well-known in wooden boat circles. He has written a book on the boat building methods employed in the Herreshoff yard in the 19th century. The book is regarded as the standard text on the subject. I have read it; it is somber and highly technical. He is married to a woman named Miranda. Miranda is an art teacher at a nearby high school. They have a son, Edward, who at this writing is fourteen, about the age that Keefer went off the rails for the balance of his adolescence. Let's hope history doesn't repeat itself.

I went to see my estranged grown-up boy when I thought the coast was maybe clear of any lingering bad feelings he might have about our last encounter and my subsequent desertion; although I knew from experience sometimes injuries like that can never be mended. The lady at the gate pointed me in the direction of the boat-building workshop and I walked over there, passing the black-hulled *Joseph Conrad* tied up at the dock. There he was, somebody I didn't recognize, doing something I knew nothing about. He had his long dark hair tied back from his face and wore a neatly trimmed, rather Victorian-looking beard, and a carpenter's apron covered with wood dust. The steel-rimmed round lenses of his glasses glinted in the sunlight as he looked up. He was a handsome, sturdy-looking man, I must say.

"Keith Gagliano?" Linda had told me he had taken her family name. A mistake, but there it was.

"Yes?"

"Hello, Keefer."

"Dad?"

"Hello, son."

CHAPTER | TWO

For the last two years, I have been invited to have Thanksgiving dinner with Keith and his family. Linda and Wesley fly in for Christmas. Although we are also invited, I always say we have other plans.

He and his wife Miranda bought an old rundown house in Mystic at the time of the real estate meltdown in 2008. Keith, with his gift for carpentry, has fixed it up and it's a beautiful little place. They live simply. He says they wouldn't even own a car (a little Subaru; everybody in New England seems to drive one) if Miranda didn't need it to get back and forth to her teaching job. He either rides his bicycle, or walks to work. You wouldn't take him for a trust fund baby. Phil set one up for him in the first year of his life, and Keith is a wealthy man, but you would never know it.

Eddie seems like a nice kid. Last time I visited, he showed me the half hull model to scale of a Friendship Sloop that he made in his dad's workshop. It is a beautiful model, layers of varnished basswood and mahogany, mounted on a varnished piece of cherry wood.

"Really? You made this by yourself?"

"You bet, Grandpa."

Grandpa. That's a good one.

He is planning to build the real thing with his father next summer. It looks like he is going to follow in his dad's footsteps without going through all the missteps. I fervently hope so.

Nola finally decided to move out of Pennsylvania. She never liked the place. Too many Germans, she said. I thought she would dart for Maine, but her old bones led her to a retirement community south of

Tampa. Shortly afterwards, she met and married a man named Lyle Puckett. Lyle has a nice pension from the Ohio Turnpike Commission. He got her interested in going to the community gym, which amazed me because she had always hated anything that made her sweat. Then, wonder of wonders, she joined the over seventy ladies' softball team and became one of the ace pitchers in the league. It was hiding in the genes all the time, and helps explain where Richie got some of his extraterrestrial abilities. Certainly it wasn't from Ray. Lyle also got her interested in volunteering at a nearby women's prison. She helped several of the prisoners with their reading. Lyle taught them how to crochet. It was a skill he'd picked up from his mother when he was a child on her farm in Nebraska during the long winters. Soon these female malefactors had brightly colored spirals of crochet on their collars and cuffs and circling the bottom their pant legs. They had a lenient warden who didn't make a fuss about them "defacing" their government issued clothing to make it a little prettier. That little bit of color on their clothes did a lot to lift their spirits.

Nola died last year at age ninety-two, forty pounds lighter and in the best shape of her life (except for being dead) and apparently the happiest she'd been since attending Richie's high school football games. Lyle was obviously the best thing that had walked into her life since those heady days of her Apollo's ascendency. It was another lesson in how a good relationship makes you want to live and have a good time.

I took a page out of Nola's playbook and moved—not to Florida, but back to Maine. I remembered being happy there as a child; but the Maine I got was not the Maine I remembered. That Maine was gone forever. There is a heroin epidemic going on among the young down on the coast, but not so much where we are in the western mountains of the state. I understand it is even worse in New Hampshire. Still, it was good. Maine was good; beautiful country, even if the people were fucked up.

A philosopher (or a quack, take your pick) named Wilhelm Reich came aground up here on a mountain top in the nineteen forties where he discovered something he called Orgone in the atmosphere;

he built Orgone Collectors, boxes made of wood and metal, something like old-fashioned steam closets. You sat in these things and let the Orgone particles penetrate you and the particles supposedly cured everything from arthritis to cancer as well as renewed your sexual energy. Eventually the Feds threw him in prison where the poor man died, totally out of Orgone. I think what he discovered was fresh air and just got carried away by it. Do you know that a young pine forest is virtually germ-free? The needles give off some kind of chemicals to protect the trees from possible invasions of bacteria. Most of the land on our forty-acre farm has reverted to new growth pine. I walk in the russet carpeted alleyways between the trees every day and I always come back to the house feeling refreshed. I'm convinced, like Reich, there is something in the air up here that makes it a particularly healthy place to live, but I won't call it Orgone. Just wonderful pine-smelling fresh air. Beautiful.

The farm was Loreen Lent's idea. Loreen and I ran into each other one day in the parking lot at the supermarket. That is to say, I backed my Opel into her Volvo. As we exchanged insurance information and telephone numbers, we got to laughing at each other's jokes, and I asked her out for a drink. Thirty-six hours later, she moved in; I thought the arrangement was temporary (what isn't?), even her name suggested it was, but somehow that was ten years ago. When I started talking about moving to Maine, she got excited and wanted to tag along. She was raised on a dairy farm in upstate New York. She is a good-looking redhead in her late thirties with a lot of energy and a droll sense of humor. I bought her some goats when we moved here and she quickly became a cheese maker extraordinaire; she sells her products at the farmers' markets both in Rangeley and in Farmington. I have taken up painting, something I used to do as a kid. It seems an age appropriate thing for an old reprobate to be doing in his declining years. One of the bedrooms serves as my studio, and I have a sign down by the road; occasionally, I astonish myself by selling one of my works to a passing fool.

Last spring, Loreen planted a vegetable garden. I built the raised beds and helped her haul the alluvial muck she wanted from the bottom of the creek near our house. She said it would really make the garden grow, so we carried buckets of the stuff back to the house and mixed it in with the topsoil and finished by spreading some more as a top dressing, and the garden seemed to spring alive over night. It was an unusually hot summer for our part of the country, but she watered everything faithfully and we had a bumper crop through the late summer and fall. We harvested lettuce of three varieties and luscious red tomatoes; she castled a dozen sprouted potatoes in mounds and suddenly we had more potatoes than we knew what to do with, along with plenty of corn and green beans, and all the herbs I use for cooking: parsley, basil, sage, dill, thyme, oregano, little trees of rosemary. The blueberry bushes she planted yielded berries a little bigger than bee-bees, like the wild kind I remembered picking with my grandmother when I was a boy. They were delicious, just perfect. She took baskets of her vegetables and blueberries to the farmers' markets and sold them along with her several varieties of goat cheese.

Loreen has a natural gift for growing things. She says she inherited it from her father; it was on his farm and in his garden that she learned what to do, but I thought it went deeper than that, not so much a learned thing, as a gift. Plants opened up and flowered for her as though she had touched them with a magic wand. As stupid as it sounds, she loved her fruits and vegetables and they loved her back. I gave her a gold pin of an angel holding a spade, a gardening angel, (a guardian angel, get it?) which seemed only right and proper for her to wear as a badge of honor for all the wonderful things that flourish under her hand.

She has the same effect on people, how quickly she makes them smile and makes them friends as she hands them a basket of flowers or some carrots or pole beans. She's made the old farm house glow, too, transformed the rooms with fresh paint and a few new furnishings, flowers from the garden in every room, making the house itself feel like one of her living things.

When I shut it down for the night, I watch her face on the pillow beside me. She's as beautiful as the woman in the Botticelli painting, the famous beauty, Simonetta Vespucci. Look it up; I kid you not. What's more, and more importantly, she's good—a good person, the best I've ever known. She sleeps on, undisturbed by the light from the lamp on my night table. I watch the rise and fall of her untroubled breathing, and I think how lucky I am.

Loreen and I lead a nice quiet life, no high drama, and not many Italians around to disturb my peace of mind. Everyone in my new town calls me "Early." My old name, Earl, that I never liked, is dead and gone. "Early" fits me better than "Steve," the name back in college that I thought I would adopt when I grew up, but Early is the right one. Nola used to call me that, but only fitfully. I'm Early Bogwell now, a good name for a hayseed, and I like it. It's helped smooth out the knots in my personality, if not in my history.

I am reminded of Plato's Myth of Er (Er, so close to "Ur") in which the dead, who have spent 3,000 years cycling through every life form, now line up to select their next try at being human beings. Ulysses is the last to select. He picks the most obscure life he can find in the most obscure family in the most remote part of Greece, because he says the last thing he wants is a lot of excitement this time around. I certainly sympathize with that point of view.

Keith and his family stay with us for a week every winter when they come up to go skiing at Saddleback Mountain. I make a big pot of cassoulet and throw in some duck confit and some ham hocks and whatever else I have around, and they really dig in after a day on the slopes. We usually have venison that one of our neighbors has given us. I make a roast with baked potatoes and a salad of winter greens and onions. Baked beans and that cabbage salad that Ray used to make is another big favorite on our menu.

They spend a week with us in the summer, too. Last year, we rented canoes and went out on the Kennebago River in search of wildlife. There is a tremendous number of moose in the woods around here, and Eddie is absolutely fascinated by them. On this trip, one of them practically got into the canoe with us.

"Wow!" said Eddie. "Did you see the size of him, Grandpa? That was the biggest ever!"

Grandpa, Loreen later whispered to me when we were fixing dinner. *That's a good one,"* and pinched my backside as she carried a casserole to the dining room table. She makes me laugh, that girl.

Linda and I still occasionally check in with one another. When you have children with someone, it's a connection you can never break even though you might like to. In one of our recent conversations she told me that Mario sold everything on the Island and moved to Connecticut. There was some lingering unpleasantness with the people at Kennedy International over something that happened thirty years ago. Some people really hold a grudge. If they tried to hold their breath like that, they'd all be dead. To misquote Linda, if you're missing ten million dollars, and you know some Italians, you automatically think they did it.

She says he owns a wildly successful seafood restaurant in Hartford called The Jolly Lobster. Good for him. She says she'd like to see him married with a family, but she doubts that he'll ever find anybody who can put up with him. I didn't think that was a very generous thing to say, but then I remembered she insults people as a way of showing her affection.

"What happened to the Vermeer?"

"What? The veneer? What are you talking about?"

"The painting in your father's dining room."

"Oh that. When he moved, I told Mario to put it out with the trash. It's ugly, it's old-fashioned, what good is it? It's little; you can hardly see it. But he likes it, so he took it with him."

"I'm happy to hear that."

"Yeah, he's got glossies of Frank, Dino, Tony, and Vic framed over the bar and that dumb painting right in the middle. I think it looks stupid. It's not right for a bar. I told him he should go for a big nude, give the guys something to look at while they sip their bourbon. Something classy like that."

"Right. Mario never did have good taste."

She told me Cousin Vito was invited to go along to Connecticut, but decided to move in with his ancient sister in Ossining. She has a garden. Maybe that was the attraction. He must be ninety by now.

What is she? A hundred? She said she missed her father. A lot of juice went out of her life when he died.

"He was so good to me. Such a handsome man! He had such beautiful hair–and that moustache! It made him look like Errol Flynn, didn't it?"

"What are you talking about? Phil was a little gimpy guy with a bald head."

"He had a limp, sure, but that walking stick with the silver dragon's head made him look so dignified. Those beautiful suits he used to wear–"

"I never saw him in a suit. He didn't use a stick. He walked up and down like he was riding on a Merry-Go-Round."

"You've lost your mind. But then how can you lose something you never had?" After a thoughtful pause, she added, "Maybe you weren't around in those days. Maybe I'm remembering him when I was a little kid. He was so kind to me! Such a beautiful man! And that moustache!"

The woman is delusional, but how else can we hold on to someone we've loved and lost? I approve of being delusional with all my heart.

A propos of nothing, she once said to me, "You know, if we were in Sicily, we'd still be married, like God and Daddy intended. People don't quit over there, the way they do in this country."

"God and your father are interchangeable entities in Italy, aren't they?"

"What are you talking about?"

"Forget it. So we'd still be together, spitting in each other's soup, and hating each other's guts, until death do us part in the old country, right?

"Yeah, how tragic. Get out your violin and set it to music."

"Right. Suffer the torments of hell, to satisfy Church and Daddy. I'd rather drive a spike into my head."

"That's a hell of thing to say. Take it back."

"You're happy, aren't you?"

"Very."

"Well then."

Notice she didn't ask if I was happy. Sometimes I wonder if this new life I've constructed is a dream. I know a hunter who tells me he's seen wolves up on the Canadian border. Wolves haven't been in this part of the country for centuries, but they're making a comeback in certain places; more and more of them are being spotted all the time. What if sometime when I'm walking in the woods I come face to face with a big wolf? What if someday Gino, the mechanic, steps out from behind a tree; and far away, down by the road that runs in front of our house, I see a limousine idling by the side of the ditch and Donkey Man leaning against the car, waiting for Gino to complete his errand? What if the back window is open just enough to allow a blue snake of cigar smoke to curl into the air and poison my germ-free pines? What if I don't know who's dead and who's alive anymore? Come on, somebody. Lie to me.

More highly praised novels by David Small

Almost Famous

The River in Winter

Alone

More of Everything: A Love Story

Keep reading for an excerpt from
<u>More of Everything: A Love Story</u>

Learn more about David Small at
davidsmallnovelist.com

Write to him at
Facebook.com/davidsmallnovelist

MORE OF EVERYTHING: A LOVE STORY

The Fox

Athree-legged fox hunted in the brush and the wind-felled trees in the field next to their house. Alan and Marilyn supposed the brush and the felled trees made good cover for rabbits and birds, and good hunting for the fox.

The fox had probably stepped into a well-disguised steel trap and had done the only thing possible to survive. He had gnawed off his leg and escaped. Now he was a three-legged hunter. Despite the disadvantage he must have had some success, for they often spotted him out their kitchen window in the field before he disappeared into the covering brush. He had a fine shiny coat of burnt orange fur, much of it pointed at the ends with black, and a fine great black brush of a tail.

They would catch him bobbing along in the tall yellow grass toward the downed trees and the underbrush two or three times in the space of a couple of weeks. They kept a look out for him from the deck or the kitchen window.

"There he is!"

Alan put his arm around Marilyn and they stood watching intently until they couldn't see him anymore.

Sometimes Marilyn would say, "Good hunting, little fox."

Or Alan might say, "Good luck, old fellow," for he liked to think of the fox as a grizzled old survivor.

This went on for some months over the summer and fall. They saw him after a heavy snowfall in December, making his way slowly to his hunting ground, and after that they didn't see him again. They talked about it one night after Christmas and the sky giving up the last of its light and no sign of the fox for weeks.

"He's a brave little fox, isn't he?"

"Yes, he is."

"You think he's all right, don't you?"

"There's a lot of building going on. They'll take the field next. He's probably moved on to better pickings."

"You're a liar, aren't you? You're a good-hearted liar," Marilyn wrapped her arms around him and held him tight.

"Poor little fox."

Later that night they were reading on the couch. He was finishing up King Lear again, getting ready to meet with his class the next day. Marilyn was looking through some old copies of Travel & Leisure. On the end table next to him, his cell phone rang. When he heard his ex-wife's tremulous voice cry out to him like a drowning person, he said, "Hold on just a second."

He covered the phone and whispered to Marilyn, "It's Kiki."

Marilyn smiled and left the room. There was no need for such discretion, if that's what it was. In fact, it worried him and made him feel rather abandoned. He watched her quietly close the bedroom door, then turned back to the phone.

"What's up, Kiki?"

"I had a call from Kenny."

"What?"

"Yes, yes! It rang! The telephone rang! I picked it up and—nothing. You know that clicking on the line you get when telemarketing computers randomly dial your number and play their tapes at you? I was just about to hang up when I heard this faint voice—you know, like you hear sometimes when the lines are crossed? And it said, 'Mom?' I distinctly heard it say, 'Mom.'"

"Kiki—"

"Listen to me, Alan! I said, 'Kenny! Where are you, baby?' And he said, 'Don't be sad, Mom. It's okay.' He said it's okay, Alan! He said it's okay!"

"Kiki, you're going through a rough time—"

"Shut up and listen, Alan! I said, 'Kenny, you don't know how much your father and I have missed you. It's torn our lives apart,' and he said, 'Tell Dad, Mom. Tell him it's okay.'"

She paused and blew out softly, "So I'm telling you."

She was waiting for his reaction to her fantastic news from the spirit world. He didn't know what to say, what comfort to offer. Kenny had been dead for fifteen years. Kiki had cancer, a bad diagnosis. The last thing he wanted to do is upset her. Mercifully she was too excited to give him time to say something stupid.

"I waited," she said. "But he didn't say anything more. Just that funny clicking sound you get on the line sometimes, but the line isn't dead, you know? Then the dial tone came on, so sudden it made me jump. I said, 'Kenny, don't go!'"

She began to cry. He shut his eyes and listened to the soft heart-broken sound. It was a long time before she was able to say in a choked voice, "So that's my Christmas miracle, Alan. A phone call from Kenny."

And quietly hung up.

It brought a lot of it back: the call at three in the morning. Sitting up out of a dead sleep. Knowing one of his boys was dead before he picked up the phone. He had kept them away from motorcycles as best he could when they were in his care but when they were with her, his rules didn't apply. He suspected that if it was something he wouldn't allow at his house, it made it all the sweeter for her to permit it at hers. She loved her boys with all her heart—yet what a foolish heart it was. She colluded with them like an irresponsible older sister, keeping Dad in the dark, in on the joke with her "little brothers," rather than acting like their mother. He could not blame her for Kenny's death. She had not slicked the roads with rain, nor told him to go riding out into the fog that night. But she had let them hide their motorcycles at her house. She let them do whatever they wanted, and she wrote off her permissiveness as love.

The poverty of the mass at Kenny's funeral came flooding back, too. The travesty of the dead religion's mumbo jumbo, the swinging incense, the old priest with his fat soft face and pursed mouth moving with difficulty under the heavy brocade of his garments, accompanied by the equally old man who looked more like an ex-convict than an altar boy. The priest's cape, the poles wagged about, the censor spewing incense, a practice originally begun by the church to fumigate the pious, because those ancient crowds stank and their rank smell offended the perfumed priests. These strangers were not even pretending that it meant anything. Why should he expect more? They didn't know Kenny. He knew it was irrational, yet he despised them because it seemed so insulting to Kenny. It would have been better had they had the body cremated and some later time held a memorial for his friends (the church was overflowing with them) celebrating what little lifetime he'd had to touch so many lives, but Kiki, her latent Catholicism revived, insisted on the whole hideous ritual.

At the grave side service under the bright blue sky in the beautiful little country cemetery that Dana had found for his brother (he was shocked that his mother was satisfied with the ugly crowded cemetery closest to her house), with the absurd canopy over the open grave and the absurd rug on the grass: more mumbo jumbo. Alan had to grit his teeth to get through it all.

He and Marilyn and Dana sat next to Kiki and her husband Bert in the front row of folding chairs, along with Alan's mother, Nina, and brother, Ben, while the priest waved his sprinkler about and muttered his obligatory incantations. When it was over, they stared at the open grave, all of them numb and unable to move.

Six months after Kenny's death Kiki called and asked if he thought God grieved for Kenny. He said that he thought in this case Kenny's family was the primary register of God's anguish.

"Case. You called it a case. You're such a cold-hearted shit."

She hung up on him then, as she frequently did.

For some reason, which he couldn't understand, the phone call was the beginning of a new pattern. From then on he could expect a call from her about every six months. Why she called him when everything he said irritated her was a mystery, but there it was: a kick in the gut twice a year. In one recent call she said she was leaving Bert and needed $400 for a security deposit on an apartment.

"Of course. But Kiki are you sure—"

"Don't try to talk me out of it!"

He'd shut up then and listened.

"I got some bad spirits around me, I swear. On the way over to the apartment I was checking out this morning, a bottle of vitamin water exploded in my car! Can you believe it? All over me! All over the seats! It knocked out my radio. At least it made it go crazy, spitting out CDs and making the volume control go bonkers. It was pumping out "Tequila Makes Her Clothes Come Off" while I'm cleaning up the car alongside the road with some towels I just bought at Macy's. All these truckers driving by were laughing and leering at my ass. I've got white slacks on and purple underwear, which probably showed through, and I guess they were having a jolly old time."

They had a good laugh over that one, but she ended up crying as she often did and hung up on him. He sent the check, but another phone call soon followed.

"I've decided to give Bert another chance. It was that exploding vitamin water that did it. Somebody was trying to tell me something."

She offered to send back the money. He told her to keep it.

"You and Bert go out and celebrate."

"Like hell. I need a new dryer."

"Good. Whatever. The point is: enjoy."

She actually said goodbye that time before hanging up.

The marriage had been bad for both of them. He found her difficult, she found him impossible. In the end all he remembered were the little things that had built up and drove him crazy. She got lipstick all over the brand new white couch. She stood in the doorway at dinnertime and called the kids home like a fishwife. She hogged the bed. She took her half out of the middle. She was impossible to move. When Dana and Kenny were babies, she slept right through when they began to howl at three o'clock in the morning. He was the one who got up and heated their bottles and changed their diapers.

He couldn't keep any booze in the house. Beer, whiskey, vodka, gin: it didn't matter what it was. She drank it up. He remembers getting a call from her one day; it was early times, before he had tenure, and money was tight. She told him to bring home a case of beer.

"I've only got five dollars until payday."

"Bring a case of beer, or don't bother coming home."

Always with the ultimatums.

Finally she pushed him too far. He had been training for a century ride on his bicycle. She'd been unhappy because every weekend, he rode for an hour, sometimes more, leaving her alone with the kids. When the day came and he was packing the car for his overnight in Johnstown, she said, "If you're going, keep pedaling."

"Good idea," he said, and that was that.

When he came for his clothes a week later, she'd thrown them out the bedroom window. They were scattered on the front lawn and hanging in the dogwood trees.

Marilyn came back into the room.

"How did it go?"

"She's had another paranormal experience. She said she's had a phone call from Kenny."

"Poor Kiki. I feel so sorry for her. Did you ask how she's feeling?"

"I didn't get the chance. She hung up on me."

"I hope you didn't upset her."

"You like her, don't you?"

"Yes, I do."

"I'm glad. It makes it a lot easier for me."

"You're pooped, I can tell. Let's go to bed."

In the morning he was still in bed as she was getting ready to leave for work. She had too much lotion on her hands and rubbed it into his forehead and temples and the crow's feet at the corner of his eyes.

"Oh, that feels good."

Then she kissed him and was gone.

He lay there thinking about the three-legged fox and the phone call from Kiki. There is so much pain in the world, yet everything is so beautiful, all the more because it is fleeting. He remembers something from St. Paul, something out of one of his letters to the Corinthians about being sorrowful, yet always rejoicing. That was, it seemed to him, the truth of the matter.

For a copy of
More of Everything: A Love Story
go to Amazon.com

Made in the USA
Monee, IL
20 May 2021